A Horse Called
Poppyseed

BOOKS BY
JoANNE CHITWOOD NOWACK:

A Horse Called Mayonnaise
A Horse Called Blackberry
A Horse Called Poppyseed

To order, call 1-800-765-6955.
For information
on other Review and Herald products,
visit our website at www.rhpa.org

A Horse Called Poppyseed

JoAnne Chitwood Nowack

A Sequel to *A Horse Called Blackberry*

REVIEW AND HERALD® PUBLISHING ASSOCIATION
HAGERSTOWN, MD 21740

The author assumes full responsibility for the accuracy of
all facts and quotations as cited in this book.

This book was
Edited by Gerald Wheeler
Designed by Willie Duke
Cover illustration by Scott Snow
Typeset: 12/14 Times

PRINTED IN U.S.A.

02 01 00   5 4 3 2

R&H Cataloging Service
Nowack, JoAnne Chitwood
   A horse called poppyseed.

   I. Title.

        813.54

ISBN 0-8280-1307-1

DEDICATION

To my parents,
Howard and Dolores Chitwood,
with love and gratitude

CHAPTER ONE

A cool morning breeze gently rattled the open blinds in the window across the room. A strange low hum filled the air. Tory rubbed her eyes, still heavy with sleep, and sat up in bed. Her long dark hair spilled over her shoulders like an unruly mop.

"What is that noise?" she muttered. Crawling out of bed, she stumbled to the window, catching her breath as she gazed out at the beautiful rolling hills of her parent's Arkansas farm. In her travels away to boarding school in Tennessee, then to Florida to work as a wrangler at Cool Springs Camp, she'd forgotten how lovely home could be.

The heavy drone grew louder, and Tory focused in on a bright red feeder hanging from a beam at the east end of the porch. A tiny jade and garnet body hovered over the feeder until a second little dynamo whirred onto the scene to chase it away. As her eyes adjusted, she could pick out dozens of hummingbirds perched on the branches of nearby bushes or darting through the air to sip nectar from the feeder.

"Wow," she whispered. "That's incredible. I've never seen so many hummingbirds in one place."

Intent on watching the birds, she didn't hear her mother's gentle knock on the door and then the creak of the hinges as she pushed it open.

"Tory, are you ready to eat some breakfast?" Dee Butler's soft voice pulled her attention from the window.

"Oh, good morning, Mom," she said, chuckling. "I was watching the hummingbirds. How did you get so many to show up?"

"Your dad's a regular pied piper when it comes to birds. Last spring he built bluebird boxes and set then up all along the north fenceline. Everyone was amazed when the bluebirds showed up to nest in them. Bluebirds have become pretty scarce in the area because all their natural nesting places have been logged over. A reporter from the paper even came one day and wrote an article about the boxes."

"And the hummingbirds?" Tory nodded toward the busy swarm of birds in the front yard. Mrs. Butler approached the window and pointed to several other feeders hanging from the porch and from tree branches.

"The secret is in keeping the feeders full so the birds trust them as a food source." She smiled. "I cook a lot of sugar water."

Tory took a deep breath as the aroma of hot biscuits filled the room. "I think I smell something else you've been cooking this morning."

"Well, come on and eat it," Mrs. Butler said, laughing. "You have a busy day ahead of you at the college. Registration starts at 10:00 this morning."

"OK. I'll be right there." As her mother headed back down the hall to the kitchen, Tory grabbed a pair of jeans and a T-shirt and slipped them on. After running a brush through her hair, she pulled it back with a cloth hair tie, then glanced around the familiar room and sighed. It was good to be home.

The kitchen table, draped in a country-print oilcloth, nestled in a corner of the kitchen just as she remembered it. She sat down at her place in front of a plate of steaming grits and scrambled eggs. A plastic bear filled with honey stood guard over hot, fluffy biscuits. Mrs. Butler placed a juice glass of fresh-squeezed orange juice in front of her daughter. Just then the front door swung open and Howard Butler's 6' 1" frame appeared in the entryway. His silver-gray hair peeked out from under a billed cap with an experimental aircraft insignia on it.

"Well, it's about time you got up," he teased. "Been up for hours myself. Got the cows moved to a new field, the garden watered, and even started a batch of bread."

Tory glanced around the kitchen and spotted a large metal bowl draped with a clean dish towel, a mound of rising bread dough bulging under the cloth. Homemade bread was Dad's specialty. Her mouth watered as she thought of the fresh, crusty loaves that would be cooling on wire racks before noon.

"Good morning, Dad," she said, smiling at her father. "It sounds like you've been busy." She slipped from her place at the table and gave him a big hug. As she looked over his shoulder out the front door, she stared in surprise. There in the barn lot, just across the gravel road from the house, stood a buckskin mare. Her tawny coat glistened in the early morning sun, setting off the jet black of her mane and tail and her four stocking feet.

Tory gave her father a questioning look. "I didn't know you had a horse."

"I don't," Mr. Butler said, grinning impishly. "She's yours. First-class barrel racer. Her name is Peaches. Isn't that some name for a horse?"

She giggled, thinking of her horse, Mayonnaise, at Cool Springs Camp. "I've heard worse. It fits her, anyway. She looks like a real peach."

"Actually, her former owner said her name is

Peaches because she loves to eat them. Would rather have them than sugar lumps." Mr. Butler pulled a peach from the big front pocket on his overalls and handed it to her. "Check it out for yourself."

Mrs. Butler sighed and slid Tory's plate of food into the warm oven. "I guess this means breakfast will have to wait."

Tory slipped her shoes on and ran down the driveway and across the road to the barn lot.

The mare flicked her ears forward, a look of intelligent curiosity in her dark eyes. She nickered softly and stretched her muzzle toward Tory as she caught sight of the peach in the girl's hand.

"You do like peaches, don't you girl," Tory whispered, holding the peach out on her flat palm. The mare took the fruit gently, licking the juice from her hand with her soft, warm tongue. Tory ran her fingers through the thick, dark mane, then down the mare's withers and across the slope of her shoulder. The muscles rippled in the horse's well-developed chest.

"A barrel racer," Tory said softly. "I bet you're fast, too."

She heard the crunch of boots on gravel in the barn lot behind her and turned to see Mr. Butler carrying a well-worn Western saddle with a leather bridle hung over the saddle horn.

"I knew you'd never be able to concentrate this morning on anything else until you had a chance to take her for a little spin to see how she handles."

She grinned at her dad. "You know me too well, you know." Reaching for the bridle, she held it out for Peaches to sniff. The mare pushed the leather aside in search of another piece of fruit. Tory slipped the snaffle bit between the horse's teeth and gently pulled the headstall up over her ears. Peaches held perfectly still while Tory fastened the throatlatch strap, sliding her hand under the strap to make sure it wasn't uncomfortably tight.

"There's something else you need to know about Peaches before you work her," Mr. Butler said, a serious tone in his voice. Tory reached for the saddle blanket her father held out to her and flipped it up onto the mare's back. She placed it high on the horse's withers, then slid it back to the correct position just behind the point of the wither bone so all the hairs on Peaches' back would be smoothed into their natural position under the saddle.

"What is it?" Tory asked as she reached for the saddle, trying to hide the apprehension welling up inside her. Was something wrong with this beautiful creature? Why would her dad buy her a horse that had a serious problem? She bit her lip as she thought of Blackberry and all the struggles she'd had with the feisty little mare during the summer. Peaches seemed so docile and well-behaved, a world apart from the flighty Blackberry. She wasn't sure she even wanted to know anything bad about the beautiful buckskin that would shatter the illusion of perfection she'd formed in her mind in just the few minutes she'd known her.

Mr. Butler stepped close to the mare's side and ran his hand along her belly. "She's due to foal in three months. Going to have a Christmas baby!"

Tory's mouth dropped open in surprise. She stared at the mare's bulging sides. Of course. Why hadn't she noticed it before?

"Maybe I shouldn't ride her, Dad. I had no idea she was pregnant."

"It's OK." Mr. Butler chuckled. "They've been riding her all along. She's in great shape. I just wanted you to know before you rode her so you'd take it easy on her."

Tory adjusted the saddle on Peaches' back and pulled the girth strap tight. She flipped the braided leather reins up over the horse's head. Leaning close to the mare's ear, she whispered, "Here we go, Mama horse. Be nice to me."

"From what I've seen of that horse, she doesn't know how to behave any other way," Mr. Butler said, standing close to the mare's head as Tory slipped her left toe in the stirrup and swung her right leg lightly up and over the saddle. Peaches never flinched or sidestepped, but stood quietly, waiting for Tory's next move.

The girl pressed the left rein against the side of the mare's neck and the horse responded by moving eagerly to the right. Tory guided her into a simple figure-eight pattern, reversing direction after several complete patterns to see how she did with lead changes. Then she pulled the mare to a stop in front of her dad.

"I can't believe how perfect she is." Tory shook her head in amazement. "How in the world did you find such a great horse?"

Mr. Butler smiled, obviously pleased with himself. "I heard about her at the cow sale last week. One of the cattlemen wanted to sell her. Seems she was his daughter's horse, and the girl went off to college. I told him I had a daughter who was coming home for college and needed a horse. So here she is."

Tory slipped from the saddle and hugged her father. "Thanks, Dad. I didn't know what I was going to do without a horse to ride this school year. I should have known you'd have thought of everything." She loosened the girth strap and pulled the saddle from the mare's back, flopping it onto the top board of the corral behind her. Mr. Butler took the reins.

"I'll put her away," he said, turning her toward the barn. "You've got a big day today, and you need your breakfast."

As Tory ran up the driveway to the house she could see her mother watching from the living room window, sipping a glass of orange juice. The girl smiled to herself. She knew a tall glass of cold orange juice would be waiting for her beside her breakfast plate. Dee Butler believed there wasn't a challenge in life that one couldn't surmount after a glass of orange juice. The thought of registration popped into Tory's mind. She'd been positive when she had talked to LeAnne about taking nursing in college that it was exactly what she wanted to do. Now she wasn't so sure.

What if I can't make it through the program? What if I faint when I have to give a shot? How can I be sure this is what God wants me to do with my life?

She tried to picture Mike sitting by the campfire at Cool Springs Camp, talking to the kids. What would he say to them about making really big decisions in life? Tory wished fervently that he was here to talk to now.

The front screen door swung open and Dee Butler stepped out onto the porch, soft blue slippers on her feet. She held a glass of orange juice out to Tory.

"Come on. You're going to be late if you don't hurry."

Tory took the glass and drank it down, then grinned at her mother. "There. Now I'm ready for anything."

"Not quite, young lady," Mrs. Butler said in mock severity. "You have a plateful of food in the house that wonders why you abandoned it."

Tory laughed. "You'll just have to tell it that where Tory Butler is concerned, horses always come first."

CHAPTER TWO

A long line of students snaked out the door of the college financial aid office and halfway down the hall of the administration building. Tory sighed and took her place at the end of the line. She knew her parents could never afford to send her to college if it weren't for scholarships and grants. But she hated all the questions she had to answer on all those long, boring forms.

"Hey, I haven't seen you around here before."

Tory looked up to see a slightly-built young man with sandy blond hair and a mischievous grin waving at her from his place ahead of her in line. He wore a bright-blue shirt that matched his eyes perfectly and a white Panama hat with a black band. She ignored him and pretended to leaf through the notebook in her hands.

"Where are you from?" This time the voice came from right beside her and Tory realized the young man had given up his place in the line to stand with her. She tried to look nonchalant, but something about those intensely blue eyes unnerved her.

"Uh, Florida, sort of," she said, feeling foolish for stuttering and wondering how her hair looked. Caught up with thoughts of Peaches and her future foal, Tory had forgotten to even look in the mirror before she left the house.

"What do you mean, sort of? How can you 'sort

of' live somewhere?" Mr. Blue Eyes asked, watching her intently.

"Are you always this shy?" Tory said, an edge of annoyance in her voice. "I've never even met you and you're asking me personal questions."

"Oh, sorry." The young man stuck his hand out to shake Tory's. "I'm Kane Austin. Studying to be a teacher. Pilot, poet, dreamer of dreams, and astute observer of beautiful young women who have obviously arrived here from distant places."

She took the offered hand and shook it. "Hi, Kane. I'm glad to meet you. I'm Tory. And I am sort of from Florida and sort of from Arkansas and sort of from Alaska and lots of other places, too. My dad was in the Coast Guard before he retired to Florida several years ago. When he got tired of the heat and the rattlesnakes and the mosquitos, we moved to a farm in Arkansas. There, now you know more about me than you wanted to."

Kane laughed and shook his head. "On the contrary. I'd like to know much more. I could take you flying sometime. Would you like to go?"

"Next." A woman from one of the offices stood in the doorway and motioned to Kane. Tory was startled to see that he was the next person in line. She had been so intent on their conversation that she hadn't even noticed the line moving.

He leaned toward her before he turned to follow the woman into the office. "I'll find you, Tory. Think about it and we can talk later, OK?" He reached out to shake her hand again. "Is it a deal?"

She shook his hand and laughed. "You are a very persistent person, aren't you?"

"You haven't seen anything yet." Kane tossed his Panama hat into the air, catching it with his head, then winked at her as he disappeared into the financial-aid office.

The rest of the morning sped by in a blur of financial-aid forms and class scheduling. Tory shuddered as she studied the lineup of classes she'd be taking this term. Nursing classes and clinicals dominated her day, but she'd had to squeeze anatomy and physiology and a speech class into her schedule since she hadn't taken them last year. She sat down on a low stone wall outside the administration building to catch her breath and fight the wave of panic that threatened to overwhelm her.

Father, I don't know what I'm doing here, she prayed. *I can't do this without you. Please guide me.*

Tory looked up to see a young woman in a denim jumper walking down the steps from the administration building, a stack of books in her arms. Her shoulder-length black hair hung in soft curls around her face. The girl paused as she reached Tory, her brown eyes lighting up as she saw the nursing textbooks stacked on the wall beside her.

"Oh, you must be in the nursing program too."

Tory smiled as she looked up at the girl. "I am. But I'm feeling pretty intimidated by it right now."

The girl rolled her eyes. "Me too. All these books. And I made the mistake of looking through some of them. I don't know how I'm ever going to learn all this." She sat down on the wall beside Tory. "I didn't introduce myself to you. I'm Robyn."

"I'm Tory. I'm very glad to meet you. Especially since we're going to be fellow sufferers through anatomy and physiology class." She pointed to the huge book on the top of Robyn's stack with a picture of the human circulatory system on the front.

Robyn groaned. "Yes, I've been having nightmares

all week of sitting in class where everyone is busily taking notes and nodding in agreement with everything the teacher is saying, and I can't understand a word of it. The teacher is speaking Chinese or something. Do you suppose it's an omen?"

Tory laughed and shook her head. "I don't think so. I think it's probably normal college jitters. I was just sitting here praying for help to get over mine. That's when you came along, so I guess you were God's answer to my prayer."

The other girl's eyes grew wide. "Do you really think so?"

"Sure." Tory smiled at her new friend. "It worked too. I feel a lot better having company in my misery."

Throwing her head back, Robyn laughed heartily, then her expression grew serious. "Were you really praying when I walked up? I mean, can you just talk to God like that about something so silly as being afraid of school?"

"I don't think anything that's important to us is silly to God," Tory said quietly. She stood and picked up her books. "I have an appointment with my advisor in five minutes so I'd better head that way. Are you all done for the day?"

Robyn nodded. "Yep. Thank goodness." She pulled a piece of paper from her notebook, scribbled some numbers on it, and handed it to Tory. "Here's my phone number. Give me a call if you get a chance. Maybe if we stick together through this ordeal we'll both survive!"

Tory tore off the bottom part of the paper, wrote her phone number on it, and gave it to Robyn. "Sounds like a plan," she said with a smile.

After starting down the sidewalk toward the parking lot, Robyn suddenly stopped and turned back to look at

Tory. "You seem to be a believer. Hey, do you ever, like, study the Bible with other people? I'd like to get to know more about God, and that seems like a logical place to start. It appears as if you're on pretty good speaking terms with him. I used to be when I was little but got away from it." Robyn blushed, as if embarrassed by her disclosure.

"I'd love to study with you," Tory said. "There are always new things to learn, and I'd like to know more too. We can explore the Bible together. I'll call you and we can set up a time."

"Great." Robyn waved and headed for her car. Tory shifted the books in her arms and sprinted up the stairs toward her advisor's office. Her heart felt lighter than it had in a long time. It had been harder than she realized to leave Cool Springs Camp and all her friends there: Mike and LeAnne, Brian, Allie, and all the horses, especially Mayonnaise and Blackberry.

I guess I was pretty sure You wanted me here for college, Father, Tory prayed. *But I didn't really believe I was going to have a life. I should have known that's not Your style.*

When she knocked on her advisor's office door, a petite middle-aged woman with a sunny smile and short sandy-colored hair greeted her warmly.

"Come on in, Tory. I'm glad to meet you. I'm Mrs. Thompson."

Tory shook the woman's hand and smiled back. She glanced around the tiny office as she followed Mrs. Thompson to her desk and sat down in the chair she offered. A large window dominated the entire wall behind the desk. Plants of every description hung from macrame hangers, giving the office the feeling of being in a jungle. Mrs. Thompson noticed Tory's interest in the plants and laughed lightly.

"I love the outdoors, but if I have to be inside I try to bring as much of the outdoors in here with me."

Tory nodded. "I can sure relate to that. I wish I could be outside all the time." She thought of Peaches at home in the pasture and how much she'd rather be on her right now than sitting in an office. The girl pictured herself riding Peaches on a mountain trail, her leather saddlebags packed with trailmix and dried fruit and a bedroll tied tightly behind the cantle of her saddle. As she urged the mare up a steep incline, she topped the crest of a hill to see a sapphire blue lake stretched serenely before her in the valley. Lofty evergreens rimmed the lake like sentinels guarding a treasure. The scent of pine and delicate wildflowers drifted on the cool breeze . . .

"Tory, have you heard anything I said?"

Pulling herself back to reality, Tory felt her ears grow hot. She liked Mrs. Thompson, and it was embarrassing to get caught daydreaming.

Mrs. Thompson gave her a sympathetic look. "It's OK . Just don't check out on Mr. Maynard in anatomy and physiology class."

Straightening in her chair, Tory gave Mrs. Thompson her full attention. "I'm sorry. I was thinking about my new horse. I just got her this morning, and I was a little distracted. It won't happen again."

"Hey, don't worry about it. Tell me about her." Mrs. Thompson leaned forward slightly. "I've always wanted to have a horse. You're really fortunate to have a place to keep one."

Pleased that her advisor was interested, Tory found herself telling her all about Peaches and her pregnancy and even formulating a plan for setting up barrels in the field behind the barn for working the mare in the evenings after classes.

"I'd love for you to meet my daughter," the older woman said finally. "She's inherited my fascination with horses, but, unfortunately, neither of us has ever had the opportunity to follow up on the interest. You probably will meet her soon, because she's taking nursing with you. Her name is Robyn."

"Does she have shoulder length dark hair?" Tory asked. "If so, I just met her in front of the administration building before I came here." She pulled the scrap of paper from her pocket. "Is your phone number 679-4032?"

Mrs. Thompson laughed. "Yes, it is. So Robyn already found the horsewoman in the class. I might have known." She pushed an open notebook over where Tory could look on with her and pointed to a page with Tory's name on it. "I guess we'd better talk about your classes now and save some of the talk about horses for later, when Robyn and I have you over for dinner sometime. That is, if you'd like to come."

"Sure!" Tory grinned broadly. "I'd love to. Just let me know when."

"Great!" Mrs. Thompson said. "I'll talk to Robyn, and we'll figure something out. In the meantime we need to set a date for you to take your skills test. How does next Saturday sound?"

"Uh, that won't work for me. Isn't there a weekday the test is offered?"

Mrs. Thompson checked her calendar. "Nope. Only on Saturday. You need to do it this time or you won't be able to continue in the nursing program. It's required." She looked at Tory quizzically. "Is there something I can do to help you get here to take it?"

Uncomfortably Tory shifted in her chair. Mrs. Thompson had been so nice that the girl hated to create a problem. She took a deep breath. "I'm sorry, but if I have to have the test on Saturday, I won't be able to take it at all. I keep Saturday as the Sabbath, and I don't do any work or school things on that day. Is there any way at all to get a test date for me during the week?"

Mrs. Thompson looked as if Tory had just told her she'd arrived in a space ship from Mars to attend college with the earthlings. She swallowed hard, obviously buying herself time before she answered. "W-well," she said slowly, "I can take your request to the dean of students and see what he says."

CHAPTER THREE

Tory felt her heart sinking as she drove her little Datsun station wagon back along the curvy narrow roads to her parents' farm.

What if I can't get into the nursing program? What will I do then?

She thought of Mrs. Thompson's look of surprise when she realized that Tory would let herself forfeit the nursing program rather than go against her conscience in dedicating the Sabbath hours to God.

She must think I'm crazy, Father! And maybe I am. Her stomach felt like a tight knot, and her head started to ache. Then a memory from Cool Springs Camp flashed into her mind. She pictured Mike seated on a big rock in the woods behind the airstrip, where staff and campers had gathered for a Sabbath afternoon drama. He was dressed in tattered rags, acting out the part of a Waldensian hiding in the Alps from the king's men, who had orders to kill anyone daring to go against the established church.

In his role as an illegal teacher of Bible truth, Mike stood up and spoke to the little group gathered around him.

"Brothers and sisters," he had said, his voice soft at first, then growing stronger with conviction. "Truth is not worth living for unless it is worth dying for. How could we find these precious gems from God's own hand and give them up for safety and comfort and a soft life free of trials?"

He held a sheaf of dog-eared, dirt-smudged papers up for all to see, then sat back down, hugging the precious bits of hand-copied scripture to his chest. Quietly he began to sing an old hymn, "Give me the Bible, star of gladness shining, thy light shall guide me in the narrow way . . ."

Tory felt hot tears spring to her eyes with the memory. The story of the Waldensians and their courage had always touched her heart in some strange, unexplainable way. And watching Mike and the other staff act out their experience had made it seem so real that Tory almost felt as if she'd been there hiding in those mountain caves with them.

Even missing the opportunity to go to nursing school would be a small price to pay for doing what I believe is right. Especially when compared to those valiant Waldensians and their willingness to give up homes, jobs, and even their lives to stand for truth.

Tory sighed. She thought of Mike and Brian and how much she missed them. Life at Cool Springs Camp had been filled with challenges, but, even so, it was comforting to be in a place where certain principles were taken for granted. Here in a public college, those beliefs appeared foreign and out of place.

Father, help me to honor You through my actions, she prayed.

Dee Butler stood in the carport hanging heavy wet overalls on a plastic clothesline as Tory drove into the yard.

"Hi, Mom," Tory yelled out the car window. "I'm all registered, except I may not be able to take nursing."

"W-what?" Mrs. Butler dropped a pair of overalls into the grass, not bothering to pick them up. She reached the car before Tory could even open the door. "Why?"

Tory shared with her the conversation she'd had with Mrs. Thompson. "I'm sure I did the right thing, Mom. But I keep thinking about all those people I could help if I was a nurse. What if this keeps me from getting my degree? How can I help them then?"

She got out of the car and slipped her arm around her mother's waist. "Is life always this confusing?"

Mrs. Butler smiled wryly. "Sometimes it's worse." She steered Tory toward the house. "One thing you can be absolutely sure of, though. If you put God first in all your decisions and honor Him, He will honor you and give you something special to do for Him. Guaranteed."

Several hummingbirds swooped away from the feeders on the porch as Tory trudged up the steps and held the screen door open for her mother. She turned to watch the avian acrobats dive and flit back to the feeders as soon as they made certain that Tory and her mom were not a threat.

"Oh, I almost forgot." Mrs. Butler pulled a slip of paper from the pocket of her sundress. "You got a phone call just a few minutes before you drove in. From someone named Kane Austin. Anyone you know?" She raised her eyebrows slightly.

Blushing, Tory took the paper and stuffed it into her jeans pocket. "I just met him today at school," she said, not sure whether to be flattered or annoyed. "He's kind of persistent."

Mrs. Butler laughed. "He sounded nice. You'll have to invite him over."

Tory have her mother an exasperated look. "Am I being ganged up on here?"

"Of course not," Mrs. Butler said in a teasing voice. "Would I do that?" She disappeared down the hall, but Tory could still hear her chuckling softly to herself.

Tory stared at the phone on the wall, thinking about Kane and his bright-blue eyes. Suddenly a longing to see Brian welled up inside her, so strong it was almost a physical pain. She could see him clearly in her memory, sitting casually on Bullet's muscular back as the horse pranced down the trail. His rich baritone voice echoed in her mind singing a camp version of "Amazing Grace."

Brian, Brian, Brian, she thought. *Did I do the right thing when I said no to your marriage proposal? Everything here is so new and different. I'd love to be back on Mayonnaise or Blackberry riding the trails with you.*

Turning away from the phone, she kicked off her tennis shoes and replaced them with riding boots, then headed outside to check on Peaches. She could see the buckskin mare grazing contentedly in the field north of the barn. The horse, clearly expecting a treat, lifted her head and watched with her ears forward in interest as Tory climbed through the fence and walked toward her.

"I'm sorry girl," Tory said as she reached for the mare and scratched gently behind her ears.

If Peaches was disappointed to get an ear-scratching rather than something to eat, she never let on. Her deep-brown eyes seemed to take in Tory's every move, but with trust and interest, not in the skittish, suspicious way Blackberry had watched her in those early days of her training.

"You had some good handling when you were a foal," Tory whispered into the mare's ear. "Somebody did a lot right with you. I hope I can do as well with your baby."

Suddenly Tory felt the full responsibility of what she was taking on with the pregnant mare. It was almost as if she were choosing to adopt a child. She realized anew as she watched Peaches that how she treated the foal from birth would make all the difference in its future usefulness. Loss of trust caused by neglect or abuse could be overcome with a lot of time and painful effort, as with Blackberry, but how much better if it never happened at all.

Peaches nickered and pushed Tory's shoulder with her nose.

"OK, OK." Laughing, she patted the mare's soft muzzle. "I'll get the bridle and you and I can go for a spin. How about it?"

She climbed the wooden gate that led into the cool, dark interior of the barn. The smell of musty hay and old leather filled her nostrils as she pried open the creaky old door to the tack room. A huge spiderweb stretched across one corner of the room, a hapless fly caught in its sticky strands.

"Well, George," Tory called to the brown spider poised at the edge of the web, "looks like dinner is served." The spider skittered across the web and started wrapping his silken thread around the fly.

Another fly buzzed around Tory's face as she reached for the saddle hung on the rack in another corner of the stall. She brushed it away. "Go play in the spiderweb and leave me alone," she said in annoyance. Then she waved an arm toward the spider. "And thank you, George, for your contribution to society. You may have all the flies on the planet with my compliments."

Tory squinted in the bright sunlight as she emerged from the barn with a bridle hung over her shoulder and the saddle and saddle blanket clutched in her arms. The saddle blanket was a bright Indian print. Bold blue and red patterns danced over its surface like the footsteps of an old warrior. She smiled. How appropriate that her father, with his Native American heritage, would choose such a blanket for his daughter's horse.

Peaches stood just outside the barn entrance. Tory slipped the snaffle bit between her teeth and pulled the bridle's headstall up over the horse's head and behind her ears. She fastened the throatlatch, then "ground-tied" the mare by dropping the reins to the ground. A well-trained horse, Peaches would never move as long as those reins hung down.

She brushed Peaches' silky tan coat with her outstretched palm, making a mental note to buy a curry comb the next time she drove past the farm supply store. A hoof pick, a grain bucket, and a mineral block would complete her "needs" list.

The brightly colored saddle blanket looked stunning on the buckskin mare. Tory almost hated to cover it up with the saddle. But the saddle itself was a thing of beauty in its own right. Dark hand-tooled leather covered the horn and pommel of the saddle. The seat was a lighter, fine-grained leather, soft and supple. Fancy stitching lined the rim of the cantle and the edges of the stirrups.

"Whoa, girl," Tory said, stepping back and whistling in appreciation when she had the saddle in place. "You are quite the sight for sore eyes." She smiled as she thought of how many times she'd heard Mike use that phrase back at camp.

Tory tightened the cinch, then walked Peaches around in a small circle several times to get her to let her breath out. Then she tightened the cinch another several inches.

"You're a sweetie," she cooed to the mare, "but you

hold your breath just like the rest of them to keep me from tightening your cinch."

With the saddle snugly in place, Tory flipped the reins up over the mare's head and slipped the toe of her boot into the left stirrup. With a little bounce on her right foot, she vaulted lightly up into the saddle.

Tory could feel Peaches' body tense in response to the pressure of her legs. Loosening the reins, Tory leaned forward slightly. As she made a soft "clucking" sound, the mare shot forward. Tory hunkered down in the saddle and gripped with her legs.

Responding to Tory's urging, the buckskin flattened out into a dead run over the hayfield and across the creek into the upper pasture. White-faced Hereford cows with their calves scattered, bawling in fear, as Peaches bore down on them with hooves flying.

As the pair topped the ridge at the north end of the farm, Tory swung the horse to the right and slowed her to an easy canter. She patted the mare's sweat-drenched neck.

"You are the cream of the crop, young lady," she said, proudly. "I don't know how I got fortunate enough to own you, but I'm certainly not complaining. Now you've shown me how fast you can run, let's take it easy for a while and get to know each other."

With barely a touch of the reins to Peaches' neck, Tory guided the horse around the edge of the marsh that lay beyond a large pond in the northeast pasture. Cottonwood trees lined the banks of the pond, casting their reflections on the rippling water. A wood duck flew straight up out of the cattails just in front of them. Tory held her breath, tensing her body for the horse to spook, but Peaches never flinched.

As they scrambled up a small bank at the edge of the

pond, Tory pulled Peaches to a sudden stop and stared in horror. There in the water, just beyond a half-submerged log, lay a cow. Tory recognized her as Old Scarface, one of her dad's favorite cows. Apparently, from the tracks on the bank, the cow had come to the pond for a drink and lost her footing in the slippery mud. The fall must have broken her leg, preventing her from getting up, and she'd drowned. It looked as if she'd been dead for at least a day.

Tory choked back a sob and turned Peaches away. She knew her dad would need to know about Old Scarface right away. A decomposing body in the pond would poison the water for all the other animals.

A weak bleating sound from the bushes beside the path caused Tory to pull Peaches up short. Dismounting, she dropped the reins to the ground.

"Stay put, girl," she whispered. "I need to check this out."

Quietly, Tory crept toward the place where she had heard the sound. She parted the brush and found herself face to face with a tiny calf, so weak with hunger he couldn't even stand up.

"Oh, you poor, poor baby." She touched the velvety soft muzzle. The little calf struggled to get up, his eyes wide with fear, but his legs were too weak to support his weight. Tory crawled to his side and wrapped her arms around his warm body. Hugging him close and holding his legs together so he couldn't struggle free, she staggered out of the bushes to Peaches' side.

The mare snorted and sniffed the little orphan, then stood quietly while Tory tried to get her foot up into the stirrup with the calf in her arms. The calf bleated again. Jerking his legs free of Tory's grasp, he flailed them wildly. She fell backward into the brush beside the trail with the calf on top of her. Sharp thorns from a thistle ripped her arms and she bit her lip as the stinging pain brought tears to her eyes.

"You little stinker." Gathering the calf in her arms again, she made sure she had a strong grip on his legs. "I'd say you have a pretty good chance for survival with the amount of spunk you have."

The calf just lay in her arms, a glazed look settling over his eyes. He made no more attempts to get free and didn't struggle as Tory draped him over the saddle, then climbed up behind him. She reined Peaches toward the house, thinking about the dead cow and wondering if it was too late for the little calf, too.

CHAPTER FOUR

As Tory approached the barn, she could see her father working out in the garden. Lush tomato plants grew as tall as his waist. Sweet peas twisted their tendrils in an upward spiral around thin stakes, and raised cucumber beds lay thickly green beyond the potatoes. Mr. Butler looked up when he heard the slowly measured hoofbeats of Peaches' approach. When he saw the furry bundle she carried, he dropped his hoe and ran toward her.

Reaching the mare's side, Mr. Butler reached up and carefully lifted the limp calf from his place in front of Tory. He carried the animal into one of the stalls in the barn. Fashioning a soft bed of straw for the baby, he laid it down gently.

"Hurry to the house, Tory," Mr. Butler said, his voice tight. "Ask your mother to fix a bottle of starter milk. This calf needs some fluid right now if we're going to save it."

In minutes Tory returned with the bottle. She sat cross-legged in the straw, holding the calf's head up while Mr. Butler tried to get it to suck on the rubber nipple.

"Come on, little guy," Tory pleaded, tears in her eyes. "You have to try. Just drink a little."

The calf's eyes had rolled back in his head, and his breathing was shallow, like a dog panting. Tory smoothed her hand over his bright chocolate-brown-and-white coat. The fur was the softest she had ever felt.

"May I try, Dad?" she asked, shifting the calf's position so she could reach his mouth easily.

Mr. Butler handed her the bottle and nodded for her to go ahead. She tilted the calf's head and dribbled a few drops of the sticky, sweet liquid into his mouth. Poking her finger inside his mouth, she massaged his tongue, trying to stimulate the suck reflex.

Marveling at the softness of the tiny pink tongue, she dripped a little more milk into the calf's mouth. Ever so slightly the little tongue curled in an effort to suck. Tory dribbled a few more drops and the sucking motion became stronger. Gently, she slid the nipple of the bottle into place and held her breath as the calf began to pull the fluid from the bottle.

Mr. Butler grinned and gave Tory the thumbs-up sign. "Well, kiddo, I think the little guy may just make it. I hope you realize that this baby of yours is going to require a lot of feedings." He winked and Tory knew he would be as involved as she was. She traced the outline of one of the calf's delicate little ears and smiled.

"I think I'll call this little guy Mocha Mix." She pointed to the brown-and-white pattern of his coat. "Don't you think it fits him?"

Mr. Butler stood up. "I think it fits him perfectly. Now I need to go find his Mama. Something must have happened to her for her baby to be in this shape."

"I found her, Dad," Tory said, quietly. "It was Old Scarface. She fell in the pond and drowned."

Heaving a heavy sigh, Mr. Butler trudged out of the stall. Tory could hear the tractor's engine roaring to life, so she knew her father was heading for the pond to pull the cow out of the water. It was a grisly task, but she knew it was part of farm life. It almost seemed that for every new life on the farm something died. The cycle of birth and death repeated itself over and over with no apologies for the pain it sometimes caused for those involved. She repositioned the calf in her lap, watching with pleasure as he downed the last few drops of milk.

"I'll be glad when we're on the New Earth," Tory whispered to the little creature. "There won't be any death there. No more orphans like you. Won't that be great?"

The calf butted Tory in the stomach with his head. His brown eyes had lost their glazed look and Tory could see a twinkle of mischief in them. She scooted him off her lap onto the straw and watched him to see if he had gained enough strength to stand up. Within minutes the little fellow scrambled to his feet, bleating contentedly. He nuzzled her shoulder and tried to suck on the sleeve of her T-shirt.

"Hey, I'm not your mother," Tory said, laughing. "Or am I?" She thought of the new foal to be born in just a few months. "It looks like my family is growing faster than I thought it would." Pushing the calf away, she stood.

"Tory! Telephone!" Mrs. Butler's voice sounded faint and far away from inside the barn. Slipping out of the stall, Tory pushed Mocha Mix back gently as he tried to follow her. She ran down the breezeway and out into the bright sunlight. Her mother stood on the front porch, the cordless phone in her hand.

"What happened?" Dee Butler asked as Tory ran up the driveway. She had a worried expression on her face. "Why did your dad take off like that on the tractor?"

Stopping short, she stared at her mother. "Peaches!" Without even asking who was on the phone, Tory turned on her heel and ran to the barn. The mare stood quietly behind the barn, her saddle and bridle still on. She nickered as Tory approached her.

"You knew I wouldn't leave you like this, didn't you?" Tory said soothingly. "I forgot to tell you what a wonderfully good girl you were to help me bring little Mocha Mix up from the pasture."

She patted the horse's neck, then loosened the girth strap holding the saddle in place. Pulling saddle and blanket off together, she hung them on the top board of the corral fence. Then she slipped the bridle from the mare's head.

"Go on, girl." She used the reins to give Peaches a friendly slap on the bottom. "Get on down to the creek and get yourself a well-deserved drink."

Dee Butler still stood on the porch with the phone in her hand and a bewildered expression on her face as Tory returned from the barn. Her daughter realized with chagrin that she'd just left her mother standing there without answering any of her questions.

"I'm sorry, Mom," she said. "I didn't mean to take off on you like that. I just forgot about Peaches, and I needed to take care of her." She shared the story of her ride on Peaches and of finding Old Scarface and Mocha Mix.

"So that's what the calf milk was for!" Mrs. Butler exclaimed. As a farm wife, she had learned long ago to do what needed to be done first and ask questions later. She held the phone out to Tory. "He's still on it. Said he'd wait for you to come to the phone. It's been several minutes now."

Tory took the phone, amazed that anyone would wait that long for someone to answer.

"It sounds like you've been a little busy," Kane's cheerful voice responded to Tory's hello. "I didn't mean to interrupt your rodeo. Your mom says you've been out riding the range."

"That isn't the half of it." Tory laughed. "If you only knew."

Kane was silent for a few seconds, then said quietly, "I'd like to know. I'd like to talk to you today. Will you go flying with me if I come and get you right now?"

Tory gulped. She loved flying. Her dad had flown small aircraft ever since she could remember and her uncle was an airline pilot. But to go flying with a guy she'd just met today? She put her hand over the receiver and turned to her mother.

"Mom, he wants me to go flying with him right now."

Mrs. Butler smiled. "So, go."

"OK," Tory told Kane quickly, before she could change her mind. "I'll go with you." She gave directions to the farm and hung up the phone.

"I don't know about this," she said, shaking her head. "He's a nice guy, but I'm not sure I'm ready for a relationship." *With anyone but Brian,* she added in her own thoughts.

Mrs. Butler shook her head. "You don't have to have a romantic relationship with someone to be friends. It will be good for you to get out and have some healthy fun. I'm glad you decided to go."

Thirty minutes later a full-sized white Ford pickup truck bounced down the gravel road and pulled into the driveway. Tory stepped out onto the porch as Kane climbed out of the cab of the truck, the white panama hat with the black band on his head and a huge grin on his face. "Hi, Tory. Great place you have here," he said, looking around admiringly. The windsock in the hay-field caught his eye. "Do you have an airstrip?"

Mr. Butler walked in from the barn just in time to

hear Kane's last question. He reached out to shake his hand. "Hi. Howard Butler's the name. And I do have an airstrip. And an airplane. Except it isn't finished yet. It's a little Canadian-designed homebuilt called the Christavia. Would you like to see it?"

Tory watched the two walk away, immersed in animated conversation about airplanes and flying. She was glad her dad had someone to talk to right now, about a subject he loved, to help get his mind off the loss of Old Scarface. Within a few minutes Kane and Mr. Butler were back, still talking as if they had known each other for years. Tory introduced Kane to her mother and took him on a tour of the barn that included George's web, Mocha Mix's stall, and the field behind the barn where Peaches grazed. She found herself telling Kane all about the day's experiences, including how she felt about finding Old Scarface in the pond. Kane's blue eyes were sympathetic as he listened.

"You've had far too much trauma for one day," he said when she'd finished. "It's time for some adventure."

The little airport was quiet when Kane and Tory pulled into the parking lot. Tory had been to it with her dad many times for Experimental Aircraft Association meetings, but coming here with Kane made it all look different. He led her proudly to a white Cessna 172 with red and black stripes down the side and helped her climb up into the cabin.

As soon as he was sure Tory was comfortable, he walked around the outside of the aircraft for a careful preflight check. She watched him run his fingers along the propeller edges, checking for nicks and cracks. He peered into the opening behind the propeller, making sure no birds had built their nests on the engine. She knew an undetected bird's nest could cause an engine fire during flight.

Reaching under the cowl, Kane drained the water that had collected from condensation in the fuel system. Then he drained some fuel from each wing tank. After cleaning the windscreen and visually checking the fuel level in the tanks, he ran his hand along the leading edge of the wing to check for any damage that might affect airflow over the wings in flight. Next he reached inside the cockpit through the window and flipped the toggle switch that controlled the flaps. Once satisfied that they were working properly, he walked around the fuselage. Tory turned around in her seat and watched him through the back window as he examined the hinge points on the elevator and rudder, and checked the fuselage for any signs of damage.

His exterior inspection complete, Kane grinned at her as he opened the door and climbed into the pilot's seat. She smiled back, but said nothing. Long ago she'd learned not to talk to a pilot in the middle of a preflight check, and she knew that the outside part was only half of the inspection. Once inside, he flipped the toggle switch again to run the flaps back up to the neutral position. He made sure the fuel selector switch was on both tanks and the elevator trim was set for take-off. Then he primed the engine, turned the master and magneto switches on, and pushed the mixture control knob all the way in to "full rich."

Pushing his Panama hat down on his head, Kane turned to Tory. "OK, girlfriend. Holler the magic words out the window for me, would you?"

Tory pushed her window open and stuck her head out. "Clear prop," she shouted as Kane turned the starter key. With a shake and a shudder, the prop began to spin. She put her hands over her ears to block out the roar of the engine. Kane shook his head in mock dismay.

"What kind of pilot are you, anyway," he shouted above the din. Closing and latching his window, he taxied the plane out to the runway. Once he reached the run-up area, he held the brakes and moved all the controls to make sure they were operating smoothly. He kept the brakes on and pushed the throttle until the tachometer read 1700 RPM. After checking the magnetos and carburetor heat, he pulled the throttle back to idle and turned the plane in a full circle, visually scanning the area.

"All set for takeoff. Are you ready?" he asked.

Tory nodded. She always forgot between flights how involved the takeoff procedure was. It would be good to finally be in the air. Kane held the radio microphone to his mouth.

"Pocahontas traffic, this is Cessna 707Lima taking off runway 34, left hand turnout." He pulled the aircraft onto the runway, lining it up on the center line. As he pushed the throttle in, the plane picked up speed. Tory watched the grass and bushes along the side of the runway become a blur as they whipped by. Reaching takeoff speed, Kane slowly pulled back on the control yoke. They were airborne!

Kane smiled at Tory as he banked the plane to the left, leaving the airport traffic area.

"Where to, sunshine. It's your call."

CHAPTER FIVE

The familiar buildings and streets of the town looked strange from the air. Tory giggled as she looked down at the little water tower that appeared so huge from the ground. The town resembled a giant sandbox filled with toy cars and buildings from some boy's play-set. Miniature cows grazed in neat patches of green pasture, and a ribbon of blue wound through the scene with tiny boats dotting its surface.

"Looks totally different from up here, doesn't it?" Kane pulled the radio headset off and sat back in his seat. Tory was surprised how well she could hear him even above the sound of the engine.

"Yeah. It's amazing. Surprises me every time." She smiled at him. "Maybe that's why I like flying so much. It's such a fresh new look at life. When I'm trying to resolve some thorny issue, it always helps to have a different perspective."

"A bird's-eye view." Kane chuckled and gave her a sideways look. "So what thorny problems are you dealing with? Do you mind sharing them?"

Tory sighed. "It's a problem with school. To get into the nursing program I have to take a test on Saturday and I can't do that, so I may not get to take nursing. I'm not sure what else to do if I'm not a nurse. It just seems kind of overwhelming to me right now to have such uncertainty hanging over me."

"That does sound a little thorny," Kane said with genuine concern in his voice. "There's just one part I don't get. Why can't you take the test on Saturday? It seems like you'd be able to rearrange your schedule for something as important as the test."

"Oh, scheduling isn't a problem," Tory said, quickly. "It's that I'm a Christian and I keep the seventh-day Sabbath like Jesus did and like the Ten Commandments say to. I love the special time I spend with God on that day, and I don't let any everyday things like work or school interfere."

His eyes widened in surprise. He was quiet for a long time before saying anything. Tory watched the little cars and trucks on the strip of highway below and didn't comment either. She was sure Kane's silence must mean he thought she was completely crazy and couldn't wait to land the airplane and let her out. But when he finally spoke, she sensed a wistful tone in his voice.

"It must be nice to have strong convictions like that to base your decisions on." He banked the plane sharply to the right and pointed down at the large metal roof of a barn. A perfectly square green patch lay just beside it with a tiny tractor parked nearby. Kane pointed to a little man dressed in blue overalls who was waving from the middle of the garden. He grinned at Tory. "Recognize anyone or anything down there?"

Tory shrieked with delight and opened her window to wave frantically at the figure in overalls. "That's my farm and my dad!" She leaned over as far as her seatbelt would allow, trying to take in the view of the whole farm at once. Peaches looked up from her grazing as Kane buzzed the barn.

"Hello, girl," Tory yelled out the window.

The airstrip in the hayfield was clearly visible from above. Kane flew over it several times, mentally calculating its length.

"I think I could land there," he said, excitement in his voice. He glanced at Tory's stricken expression and added hastily, "but not today, of course."

They circled the farm one last time, buzzing as close as they could get to the ground and still be safe. Tory could see her mother standing on the front porch of the farmhouse. She waved her apron at them as they flew over.

"Well, are you ready to head back to the airport?" Kane asked as he banked the plane to the east and began to gain altitude again.

Tory nodded. "What a great surprise!" She smiled happily. "Thanks for doing this, Kane. It really means a lot to me."

"Good," Kane said so softly Tory almost couldn't hear him above the whine of the engine. "I'm glad it did. I was hoping . . ." His voice trailed off and he stared out the window.

"Hoping what?"

Kane reached over and took her hand gently in his. His blue eyes clouded with pain for an instant, then he cleared his throat and continued.

"I was hoping we could see more of each other. I know you're a Christian, and I like your spiritual strength. I wish . . ." He paused and swallowed hard. "My grandfather was a Baptist minister, and as I was growing up I always assumed I'd walk in his footsteps and be a minister, too. Somewhere along the line, though, I realized that I didn't believe it. I can't accept Christianity. My idea of spirituality runs more along the lines of Zen Buddhism. It's not a religion, but a belief that God is in everything and spiritual truth can be found by quieting outside distractions and looking within."

Tory stared at the airplane's instrument panel. Her thoughts tumbled over each other in mass confusion. She'd never had a friend that didn't at least have a semblance of belief in Christianity. Could she have a relationship with someone whose beliefs were so different from her own? She searched her memory for information about Zen Buddhist teachings. The only recollection she had of anyone who talked about Zen Buddhism was a young man she knew in high school who had been a Christian, but became fascinated with Zen meditation practices and eventually drifted out of Christianity altogether.

"Uh, well . . . ." Tory stumbled over the words, not wanting to say anything that would hurt Kane's feelings but not sure at all how to react. After all, she hardly knew him. and he seemed to be coming on awfully fast. "I'd like to keep talking about things." *Lord, help me say the right thing here.* "I'd like to be your friend and find out more about how you believe."

Kane breathed an audible sigh of relief. "Good," he said. "I'd really like that. I think we can learn a lot from each other."

Tory gazed out the window on her side of the cabin and noticed in the distance the ribbon of pavement that served as a runway for the little airport.

"Pocahontas traffic, this is 707Lima, five miles north of the field and landing," Kane announced over the radio. As he approached the airport, he banked the plane to the right, buzzing the runway then circling around in line for a landing. Tory held her breath as the plane slowed, nose down, and the wheels hit the pavement with a screech. She knew from watching Kane throughout the flight that he was an excellent pilot, but landings always gave her butterflies. Glancing at him, she smiled as he raised the flaps and slowed the plane.

Kane taxied the plane back to the hangar and swung it around into his parking slot. Tory watched his hands moving quickly and efficiently, turning off the lights, cutting the radio, and pulling the red knob that controlled the fuel mixture all the way out to cut the fuel supply to the engine. There was sudden silence as the prop stopped spinning.

"All right." Kane grinned at her as he unfastened his safety belt. "Another uneventful landing."

Tory pinched her nose with her thumb and forefinger and blew out, trying to equalize the pressure in the ears. "Except for the fact that I still hear that prop roaring in my head." She laughed and pushed her door open. "But it's a small price to pay for such an adventure." Then she helped Kane chock the airplane wheels and fasten the tiedown chains to the rings on the lift struts and at the tail.

The sun was setting over the trees as they climbed into the pickup to head for home. Streaks of brilliant orange and pink lit up the sky. Tory gasped in wonder at the breathtaking sight.

"God is such an artist," she said softly. "Just look at that masterpiece."

Kane shifted uncomfortably in his seat. Tory glanced at his face. His expression looked pensive, but he said nothing.

By the time they arrived back at the farm, dusk had settled over the hills and Tory could see her mother in the warmly lighted kitchen preparing the evening meal.

"M-m-m, I smell cornbread," Tory said as Kane held the front door open for her.

"And beans," Kane added. "My favorite meal."

Dee Butler waved a wooden spoon toward the kitchen table and laughed. "Well, sit down you two. Supper's ready. And you're right, it's beans and cornbread."

"With my famous homemade pickles on the side." Mr. Butler emerged from the bathroom in the hall, still wiping his hands on a towel. When he saw Kane, he reached out to shake his hand, grinning broadly. "Some good flying there, son. We'll have to go up together sometime."

Kane's face lit up with pleasure. "I'd like that, sir."

The dinner conversation was lively with Mr. Butler and Kane exchanging stories about flying adventures and other outdoor experiences. Tory watched Kane as he talked. His blue eyes sparkled with enthusiasm and excitement. It was clear that her dad liked him and was enjoying his company. Mrs. Butler kept everyone's plates full, not saying much, but the slight smile on her face and the interest with which she listened to Kane's stories told Tory that her mom approved of her new friend, too.

When everyone had eaten their fill of beans, Mrs. Butler pulled a large baking dish from the oven where it had been warming. "I have some blackberry cobbler here if anyone is interested in it. There's ice cream to go with it."

Kane pushed his chair back and jumped up to take the cobbler pan from her hands. "Here, let me dish it up." He sniffed the steam escaping from slits in the flaky, golden crust.

"Wow," he sighed. "This is heaven. And ice cream, too. I can't believe it."

Mrs. Butler laughed, her cheeks flushed. She showed Kane where to find the bowls and spoons, then sat down while he served the dessert.

"Oh, I almost forgot," she said, turning to Tory. "You got a phone call from Mrs. Thompson. She said it was very important that you talk with her as soon as possible. Here's her number." She handed Tory a slip of paper with the same phone number on it that Robyn had given her that morning.

Tory stared at the paper in her hand. Sure that the call concerned her test for the nursing program, she slipped quietly from the table. "Excuse me just for a minute, please. I need to find out about this now or I won't even taste my blackberry cobbler."

After dialing the number, Tory waited for what seemed like an eternity for Mrs. Thompson to answer the phone. Finally she answered. "Oh, Tory," she exclaimed when she heard the girl's voice on the line. "I'm so glad you called. I met with the dean of the college this afternoon. He consulted with several of the nursing faculty and they're rescheduling your test for tomorrow morning. You don't have to take it on Saturday."

Tory felt hot tears of relief and gratitude well up in her eyes. "Thank you, Mrs. Thompson," she said. "You don't know how much this means to me."

A moment of silence on the other end of the line, then Mrs. Thompson spoke, her voice sober. "I can see it means a lot to you. I'd like to know more about why it means so much to you. Maybe we can talk about it sometime."

"I'd like that," Tory said.

"Well, I'll see you tomorrow. Goodbye."

Tory stood and stared at the phone in her hand. Then she ran back into the kitchen, letting out a whoop of joy. Kane and her parents looked up in surprise as she slid into her chair and buried her head in her hands, laughing and crying at the same time.

Kane handed her a bowl of blackberry cobbler with a generous scoop of ice cream on top. "Hey, Tory. Can you come back down to earth long enough to eat this? That must have been some phone call."

Tory sat back in her chair and grinned broadly. "It was. I'm still in. I get to take the test tomorrow." She shook her head in amazement. "God came through again. I'm going to get a chance to be a nurse after all."

CHAPTER SIX

Tory straightened her white nursing cap and gave her crisp navy blue and white uniform one last check in the mirror. The week following her phone call with Mrs. Thompson had sped by in a busy round of testing and orientation to her new classes. Now here she was, ready to meet her first patient for her first day of nursing clinical. Her heart pounded. How could she give nursing care when she'd had less than a week of nursing school?

When she tried to swallow, she realized her mouth was as dry as a cotton ball. Slipping out of the bathroom, she scanned the hallway for a drinking fountain.

"Oh, there you are, Miss Butler." Tory felt a hand on her shoulder, guiding her with a gentle but unmistakable pressure down the hospital corridor toward her first patient's room. She looked back over her shoulder into the kind blue eyes of Mrs. Hayes, her clinical instructor. The older woman gave her an understanding smile as she released her just outside the room. "It's OK to be nervous. We all were on our first day. Just jump in and do it. You'll be fine."

As her instructor disappeared into another patient's room, Tory reviewed her nursing duties in her mind, trying to remember some of the strange new terms she had received to memorize before coming to the hospital.

"It's a whole new language," she muttered under her breath. "This," she said, hugging the contraption she'd been given to take blood pressure with, "is a sphygmomanometer. Try saying that three times in a row."

"What's that? Who's out there talking?" The high-pitched nasal voice startled Tory, and she dropped the blood pressure cuff, barely catching it before it hit the tile floor of the hospital corridor. Taking a deep breath, she marched into the patient's room.

"Hello, Mr. Babcock," she said, glancing at the patient's name on her clipboard. "I'm Tory, your student nurse for today. I'm here to take your temperature and blood pressure." She flashed the old man what she hoped was a smile of confidence.

Sitting in a recliner chair next to his hospital bed, Mr. Babcock peered at her through thick, dark-framed glasses, a dour expression on his wizened face. "Student nurse? Hmph. Why can't they give me a real nurse for a change?" His hands rested on the arms of his chair and Tory noticed that they shook continuously as he talked.

"Well, you'll have to settle for me today," she said with more cheerfulness than she felt. The grumpy old man wasn't exactly the dream patient she'd envisioned when she pictured herself as a nurse, heroically tending to the sick and wounded. She wrapped the cuff of the sphygmomanometer around his arm and placed the earpieces of the stethoscope in her ears. As she squeezed the bulb on the cuff to inflate it, Mr. Babcock began shaking even more violently.

"Mr. Babcock," Tory said firmly, "you will have to hold your arm still if I'm going to be able to get a blood pressure reading on you. Please try." She pressed the bell of the stethoscope into the space on the inside of his elbow and tried again to inflate the cuff. The shaking continued, making it impossible for her to hear anything. "Mr. Babcock," she repeated, an edge of irritation creeping into her voice, "you must hold still."

Suddenly, Mr. Babcock reached over and jerked the cuff from his arm. "I can't hold still," he hissed. "I have Parkinsons and I have no control over the tremors. Now get out of my room and don't come back." With that, he threw the blood pressure cuff on the floor, leaned back in his chair, and closed his eyes.

Tory stood frozen in place, staring at him. She remembered now, when she took report on him from the nurse who had taken care of him during the night, that his Parkinsons had worsened. Of course he had no control over the tremors. A sense of shame settled down over her like a heavy blanket.

Mr. Babcock opened one eye and saw her still standing by his chair. "What are you doing? I told you to get out of my room," he growled.

Taking a deep breath, Tory knelt down beside Mr. Babcock's chair so she could be at eye level with him. If there was anything she didn't want now, it was to appear to be talking down to her angry patient. She placed her hand gently on his arm. "I'm leaving, Mr. Babcock, just as you requested. This is your room and you have the right to say who you want in it. But before I go I want to tell you how sorry I am that I was impatient with you and expected you to control your shaking. It must be terribly difficult to live with a condition such as you have, and I didn't mean to make it harder for you."

The old man grunted something she couldn't understand and sat unmoving, his eyes shut tight. Picking up the blood pressure cuff, she gathered her charts and clipboard and started for the door.

"Wait a minute," he said, a softer tone in his voice. "I guess you can stay and do what you need to do. I don't want you to get in trouble with your instructor."

Tory turned with a smile. "Thanks, Mr. Babcock." She placed the blood pressure cuff back on the man's arm, this time holding his arm firmly in place with her own elbow to keep it from moving so much. After quickly pumping the pressure in the cuff up, she strained to hear the little rhythmic thumping noises that let her know when to start measuring his blood pressure.

"128 over 87," she announced when she finished. "Why, Mr.Babcock, you have the blood pressure of a 25-year-old."

Mr. Babcock looked surprised and pleased. Tory reached for his right hand, tracing her finger up from his thumb to find the place on his wrist to take his pulse. She counted the pulsebeats for a full minute to make sure her measurement was absolutely accurate.

"Your pulse is 78 beats per minute. That's very good." She carefully recorded his pulse and blood pressure on her clipboard. As she glanced up from her notes, she noticed a picture of a young woman on Mr. Babcock's bedside stand. The woman's dark hair framed a round, pretty face. "That's a lovely girl in that picture," she said, motioning to the place where the picture stood.

Mr. Babcock's eyes glowed. "That's my granddaughter," he said proudly. "She just graduated from high school at the top of her class. She's studying to be a doctor."

"Wow," Tory said. "What a lucky girl she is to have so much going for her and a grandpa who loves her besides." She squeezed Mr. Babcock's hand. He pulled a handkerchief from his pocket and blew his nose loudly.

"I wish she knew how much I love her," he said, his

50

voice tight with pain. "It's been several years since I've seen her. Her parents divorced and everything kind of fell apart in the family. She lives somewhere in California with her mother. The worst of it for me is that the doctor just told me I have cancer besides my Parkinsons and I may not live more than just a few more months." He blew his nose again, his eyes rimmed red from holding back the tears.

No wonder he was grumpy when I first came in the room, Tory thought.

Just then Robyn poked her head in the door. "They sent me to get you. There's an inservice on wound care in the conference room on first floor that they want us to attend. Are you ready?"

Tory flashed Robyn a warning look, expecting Mr. Babcock to explode with anger at the intrusion, but he just sat quietly, wiping his eyes and folding and unfolding the handkerchief in his lap.

"Robyn, this is Mr. Babcock," Tory said. "He was just telling me about his granddaughter."

The man looked up at Robyn, a sad expression on his face. She approached him and put her hand on his arm. "You must really miss her," she said gently.

Blowing his nose again, Mr. Babcock straightened in his chair and motioned for the girls to leave. "You have a meeting to go to," he said. "Don't be late on my account."

The girls nodded and, with a final pat on the old man's arm, hurried out the door and down the hall to the elevator.

"What do you think about that?" Robyn asked as they waited by the elevator.

Tory shook her head. "What do I think about what?" She punched the elevator button again several times.

"Your patient. He was really upset about his granddaughter." Robyn shook her head thoughtfully. "Something just doesn't seem right to me there. Do you know the history? I just get the feeling there's more to the story than just a lonely grandfather missing his family."

Tory nodded. "There is more. I know a little of it, but we shouldn't talk about it here by the elevator where others might hear. It wouldn't be fair to Mr. Babcock."

"That's right," Robyn said, embarrassment in her voice, "the confidentiality issue. I'd forgotten. Sorry."

Just then the elevator door opened and Tory stepped back to let her friend get on first. "It's OK," she said. "There's so much for us to learn I'm sure we're both going to forget things on a regular basis. I just hope I can remember enough to make it through."

"Me, too." Robyn sighed. Then her face brightened. "Hey, speaking of learning, you said we could study the Bible together sometime. When can we get together? I've thought of a hundred questions I want to find the answers to, and I just don't know how to begin."

Tory thought quickly, mentally reviewing her week. "How about Friday night? If you want to come to my house, I can show you my new mare and the little calf we rescued. I'd love to have you meet my parents, too."

Robyn grinned. "That would be great. Friday night it is."

After the inservice, Tory returned to Mr. Babcock's floor and made a beeline to the nurses' station. A tall, slender woman with salt-and-pepper hair and kind gray eyes glanced up from her charting as Tory approached.

"I'd like to find out something about one of my patients—Mr. Babcock," Tory said.

The woman smiled. "What would you like to know? He's one of my patients on the 3-11 shift, so I just took report on him."

"I'd like to know if his granddaughter's phone number is anywhere in his record. He was crying this morning because he hasn't seen her for so long." Tory gave the nurse an imploring look. "He knows he's dying and wants to see her. Is there any way to get in touch with her?"

The woman looked startled and shut the chart she had been working on. "I wasn't even aware that he had a granddaughter. He has been almost totally non-communicative since he arrived and wouldn't share information about his personal life with any of the staff. I'll be glad to start trying to track her down. Will you be here for clinical next week?"

Tory nodded.

"Good." The nurse smiled at her. "Hopefully I'll have some good news for you when you come back."

The house was quiet when Tory arrived home after clinical. Three limes lay in the middle of the table, a small placard propped beside them with the words "lime pie kit" written on it. She laughed. Key lime pie was her dad's favorite. It would be fun to make him one for supper. A stack of mail beside the limes caught her attention. The letter on top of the stack was addressed to her and had a Florida postmark. For a moment her heart felt as if it had stopped. Could it be a letter from Brian?

She picked up the letter and turned it over. A feeling of disappointment welled up within her as she saw Breeze's name and address on the back of the letter. Then she smiled as she pictured the girl the way she'd last seen her at Cool Springs Camp, riding Midnight with Jake, her short black hair ruffling in the wind and her green eyes sparkling with excitement. Quickly she tore the letter open, eager to hear any news from Florida and the summer camp staff.

The first half of the letter was full of the latest happenings in the lives of various camp staff members. Mike and LeAnne had their baby, a boy. Someone had left the feed room door open and Merrilegs, the feisty little pony that Todd had loved so much, had gotten into the grain and stuffed himself until he foundered. Tory's eyes filled with tears as she thought of the great-hearted Merrilegs crippled up so that he'd never race down the trails again.

Allie was starting college this fall, too, studying to be a teacher. "Good for you, Allie," Tory whispered. "You'll do great."

"Guess who is studying to be a minister?" Breeze wrote. "None other than our Rob himself. And he's not the only one. I need to tell you that things didn't work out between Jake and me. He's doing well and is sticking by his commitment to Christ and plans to come back to Cool Springs Camp next year. We're still friends but I'm seeing someone else."

Tory caught her breath as she read on. "I know you and Brian had something special so I wanted to be the first to tell you instead of you hearing it from someone else. Brian is studying for the ministry and has asked me to marry him. I know it's really fast. We've only gone out for a few weeks, but I've known him for longer than that. We plan to get married in December."

The rest of the words on the page became a blur. Tory sank down onto a kitchen chair and let the letter drop to the floor.

Brian, she cried wordlessly. *This is the end for us.* A picture of him riding down the trail on Bullet's broad back filled her mind. *Oh, Father, did I ruin the plans You had for me by pushing Brian away when he wanted to be with me?* Laying her head down on her arms on the table, great sobs shook her body. She didn't even hear the soft knocking on the front door, then the hinges of the screen door creaking as someone entered the house.

CHAPTER SEVEN

Tory sat up quickly as she felt a hand gently touch her shoulder. As she turned to see who it was, she expected her mother to be standing there. But it was Kane's face she saw through the blur of her tears, his eyes clouded with concern for her.

"I'm sorry I let myself in. I hope I'm not invading your space but when you didn't answer my knock, and I could hear you crying in here, I thought I'd better check on you."

Tory wiped her face on her sleeve. "It's OK," she said, smiling wanly. "I just got some upsetting news in the mail. I'll be all right. Thanks." She stood and walked to the kitchen sink where her mother had left the clean calf bottle and the powdered milk for feeding Mocha Mix. "Would you like to help me feed my baby?"

"Sure!" Kane moved quickly to her side, watching carefully as she measured out the white powder and mixed it with warm water to fill the bottle.

Mocha Mix butted the sides of his stall and bleated with hunger as they approached with the bottle of milk. Tory held the bottle high to keep the calf from grabbing it until she was inside the stall. Then she braced herself as she offered the bottle to the animal, knowing that he could butt the bottle vigorously enough as he drank to knock her over.

"He has quite the appetite, doesn't he?" Kane chuckled as he watched the whole procedure. "And my mother says I have a hearty appetite. Except she'd never let me get away with manners like that."

After Mocha Mix had finished eating, Tory sat on the straw beside him and hugged the fuzzy calf. He snuggled against her and licked her face with his warm tongue. Kane sat on the other side of the stall, chewing on a piece of hay and watching her thoughtfully. She had to admit that his presence was comforting, especially after reading Breeze's letter.

"I came over here tonight because I wanted to ask you some questions," Kane said, finally. "I've thought about you a lot since we went flying last week. There's something different about you that I can't quite put into words. A kind of depth and purpose in your life. I want to know more about what makes you tick, why you believe the way you do. Do you feel like talking about it?"

Tory blinked in surprise. "S-sure," she said. "I'm not sure where to start. I don't see myself as having any greater depth than anyone else, but I do feel that what I believe gives me a sense of purpose. I'd be glad to share that with you."

Kane nodded and replaced the hay stalk he'd been chewing on with a fresh one. Mocha Mix laid his head down in Tory's lap and closed his eyes, content now that his stomach was full of milk. She scratched the silky place behind the calf's left ear and pondered what to say to Kane that could put words around the meaning she had found in her life since accepting Christ.

Father, help me, she prayed. *This is too important for me to just give my opinions. I need Your wisdom.*

Kane waited patiently until Tory began.

"Knowing that I'm a child of God is what gives me

a sense of purpose in life," she said. "Things eat away our peace of mind: fear, guilt, bitterness, worry, selfishness, focusing on things instead of relationships . . . lots of things, but I can say that the only way I've found any kind of freedom from them is through a relationship with God."

Kane shook his head and threw down the piece of hay he'd been chewing on. "You talk about God as if it were like a human being with feelings and emotions. I think God is much bigger than that. God is a force that's in everything, everywhere. In you, in the trees, in the rocks. I think you're limiting it by making it have a personality."

"God is more than a life force, although He is the source of all life. I know He is because of what He's done in my life." Tory leaned forward as she spoke, waking Mocha Mix up. He gave a little bleat of annoyance at having his nap disturbed, then snuggled down in a different position.

"He's changed my heart," she continued. "Changed who and what I am. I couldn't have done it on my own. I always had a feeling of emptiness, like something just wasn't quite right. Even at times when things were going well and I thought I should be happy, I wasn't. God changed that. When I gave myself to Jesus, God's Son, I felt whole and complete for the first time in my life." She shook her head solemnly. "There's no way I can explain it, but it's real. I've heard it described as 'joy.' It doesn't depend on outside circumstances, but is a sense of peace and quiet trust in God no matter what happens. And it's a gift from Him." She smiled. "Of course, I can choose at any time to take my fear and frustration back. God never forces anything on me. That's one of the things I love most about Him. He gives me the freedom to make my own choices."

Kane stared at the straw at his feet. "I wish I could believe like you do," he said. "But I can't. I can't make myself believe something I don't." He stood up and brushed the wisps of hay from his jeans. "It's getting late. I'd better go home. Thanks for talking to me." He reached out his hand. "Friends still?"

Tory took his hand and shook it. "Of course," she said, grinning. "I enjoyed our talk. Thank *you* for coming over."

As Kane pulled out of the driveway in his big white truck, he waved his white Panama hat out the window. Tory waved back and watched until he disappeared over the hill. Shaking her head, she smiled to herself . She was sure she'd never met anyone quite like Kane Austin.

Suddenly a sharp snort from the field beside the barn caught Tory's attention. Something in the tone sent chills down her spine. Sprinting toward the field, she scanned the area for Peaches, but the horse was nowhere in sight.

"Peaches!" she called, her breath coming in ragged gasps as she ran. Something was terribly wrong. She felt it.

Ducking through the barbed wire fence, she raced around to the back of the barn. There, in a pool of blood, stood Peaches, trembling from head to foot. The skin and muscle of her right hind leg were laid back from her hock to her fetlock, exposing more than 10 inches of white, shiny bone.

Cautiously Tory approached the mare. "Oh, you poor, poor baby," she murmured. "How did this ever happen to you?" She smoothed her hand along the mare's neck and down her flank, talking to her to create a continuous flow of soothing sound. She cringed as she saw the loose end of a tendon hanging from the top of the gash. It was the tendon that lifted the leg for jumping, and it was completely severed.

Tory ran to the tack room and pulled a halter and lead shank from their pegs. Her hands shook as she unbuckled the halter and placed it on Peaches' head. Then she led the injured mare slowly to a post where she could tie her up while she called for help.

It seemed an eternity until Tory saw the vet's cream-colored pickup truck pull into the barn lot. A young woman with long brown hair pulled back into a pony tail and wearing dark-blue coveralls jumped out of the truck. Tory ran to greet her.

"I am so glad to see you, Mary," she said. "It's horrible. Just horrible." She could feel tears start to course down her face, leaving hot, salty trails on her cheeks.

The vet reached out and grabbed Tory's shoulders, looking her straight in the eye. "It will be OK, Tory. Trust me. Now let's get to work."

Tory took a deep breath. "What do you want me to do?"

Mary was already pulling supplies from the back of her truck. She opened the lid of a large plastic box lined with rows of syringes and vials of medicine. Selecting a small brown vial, she plunged a large needle into the rubber top and drew out some of the clear liquid. "This should be enough sedative to calm her down so she'll let us clean out the wound." She handed Tory a bucket and a bottle of antiseptic solution. "Could you fill this with hot water and squirt some of that solution in? And we'll need paper towels and some soft rags."

As Tory ran to the house to fill the bucket, she saw her father's car turn into the driveway. He jumped out of the car just as Tory reached him. "What's going on? Why is the vet here?" he asked, his forehead furrowed in concern.

"It's Peaches. Her leg is hurt badly," she answered as she ran past him and into the house. By the time she'd filled the bucket with hot water, Mr. Butler was already beside her, grabbing clean rags from the old pillowcase hanging in the utility room where the family collected old worn-out T-shirts and other items. Tory stuck a roll of paper towels under her arm and headed for the barn lot with Mr. Butler right on her heels.

Mary stood beside Peaches as the two approached, an empty syringe in her hand. "Well," she said, "that shot should zonk her enough to let us work. It will take a few minutes though." She looked around. "I'm going to need to wash that whole leg with a lot of water before we use the antiseptic. Do you have a hose close by?"

Mr. Butler pointed to a pipe protruding from the ground near the garden spot. "There's a spigot over there with a hose on it." He hurried over to turn the water on. Tory followed him and grabbed the end of the hose, pulling it toward the spot where the injured mare stood. She could see that Peaches was beginning to get sleepy. The horse's head hung low and she leaned against the post she was tied to.

"I'm ready to start cleaning this," Mary called. "The medicine has kicked in enough, I think."

As Tory pulled the hose closer, almost reaching Peaches, but not quite near enough, she felt the hose jerk to a stop. Thinking the hose had kinked and needed straightening out, she gave it a mighty heave. Suddenly water shot straight up into the air from the spigot. It looked like one of the geysers that Tory had seen on a vacation trip to Yellowstone Park.

Mary stood beside Peaches, staring at the spouting water, her mouth hanging open in amazement. Tory felt rooted to the spot. Everything seemed to be happening in slow motion and nothing felt real. It wasn't until her dad shouted, "Get up to the house and turn off the breaker to the pump!" that she was able to move.

Within minutes, Mr. Butler had replaced the broken spigot with a new one and added a length of hose to make it long enough to reach the spot where Peaches leaned even more precariously against the heavy post. Mary gently washed the gaping wound with water. As the vet worked, Tory held the mare's head and talked soothingly to her.

"It's all right, girl," she whispered. "If anyone can fix you up, it's Mary."

Once she had the wound thoroughly cleaned, the vet examined it carefully. "I can't save the tendon," she said soberly. "But I think this will heal up as good as new otherwise, as long as it doesn't get infected." She turned to Tory. "That's where your part comes in. It will be up to you to give Peaches shots every day and clean and dress the wound." She pulled a huge thermometer from her bag and gave it to Tory. "You'll have to take her temperature daily, too, and call me if she starts running a fever."

Mary opened a package of thick black thread and pushed one end of the thread through the end of a curved needle. "Catgut," she said, grinning at Tory. Gently pulling the dangling tissues on Peaches' leg up over the bone, she poked the end of the needle into one edge of the wound and began sewing it shut. Tory watched in amazement as the vet's skillful fingers reconstructed the mangled leg.

"Is that really made from cats?" she asked, pointing to the thread.

Mary laughed and wiped her forehead with the back of her sleeve. "No," she said. "They just call it that. I think they used to use sinew from animal intestines, but that was a long time ago." She tied a knot in the thread, clipped it short, and stood to stretch.

As she waited beside Peaches, she ran her hand along the horse's abdomen, a strange expression on her face.

"Is this mare pregnant?" she asked. "She has quite the pot belly here."

Tory felt a sudden rush of fear. In all the chaos she'd forgotten about the unborn foal. "Yes, she is. She's due around Christmastime."

The vet nodded, a look of concern on her face. "Yes, she does look as if she's that far along. I hope the trauma of the injury doesn't cause her to go into premature labor."

"What can I do?" Tory asked. She felt as if someone had kicked her in the stomach. It was bad enough watching Peaches suffer, but to have her lose her baby, too, would be devastating.

Mary put her arm around Tory's shoulder and squeezed. "I know this is really upsetting to you, but you'll do fine with her," she said gently. "Keep her quiet and keep the wound clean. That's all you can do, except pray."

"I'll do that for sure," Tory said with a wan smile.

CHAPTER EIGHT

The hummingbirds were still performing their acrobatics in the dim evening light as Tory emerged onto the porch, a bottle of warm calf milk under one arm and a bundle of dressing supplies under the other. Peaches nickered from her paddock.

"I'll be there in a minute, girl," Tory shouted. "You know I have to feed Mocha Mix first. He's a growing boy, you know." She smiled to herself as she remembered how tiny and frail the little calf had been when she had carried him home on Peaches' back. Now his legs were sturdy and strong, and he could almost knock Tory down when he playfully butted her with his head. She supplemented the calf milk with feed pellets that Mocha Mix gobbled hungrily from a small plastic bucket that she kept in the barn for him.

Tory could hardly believe a whole month had gone by since Peaches' injury. The ugly gash on her leg was healing well. The horse paced the paddock restlessly, eager to be free to roam the pasture again, but Tory knew that the healing process depended on protecting the leg from flies and contaminants. No dressing would stay in place for long if the horse did very much walking. So far they had no idea as to what had caused the injury.

As soon as she finished feeding the greedy young calf, Tory turned her attention to the mare. She retrieved a card table from its storage place in the tack room and set it up in the breezeway of the barn. After she had assembled her dressing supplies on the table, she took a large syringe from a shoe box she'd brought along filled with bottles of medicine and tubes of ointment. Twisting a needle in place on the end of the syringe, she drew up 10cc's of thick white penicillin suspension from a glass vial.

"Come on, girl," Tory coaxed as she led Peaches from her stall. The mare snorted and balked when she saw the syringe on the table, but Tory offered her a chunk of carrot she'd pulled from her pocket. With a toss of her head, the horse followed the girl into the middle of the barn alley and stood quietly while Tory tied her to a crossbeam.

Just as the vet had taught her, Tory rubbed an area on the mare's neck with an alcohol pad to kill any germs. Then, using a dartlike wrist movement, she popped a sterile needle into the neck muscle and quickly attached the syringe full of medicine. Peaches jerked her head up and sidestepped as Tory emptied the stinging solution into her muscle tissues.

"I'm sorry," Tory crooned, pulling the needle out quickly and offering the mare another bite of carrot. "I know that hurts, but without it you could get very sick. Maybe you'd even lose your baby. I wish I could explain to you why I have to hurt you." She ran her hand along the horse's backbone and down her right hind leg.

Drainage had saturated the old dressing and it was dirty around the edges. Tory pulled the old tape off, releasing the soiled dressing. She examined the wound for redness, swelling, or foul-smelling drainage. When she was certain that the wound showed no signs of infection, she cleaned it with an antiseptic solution, slathered it with ointment, and wrapped it back up in a fresh dressing.

"There you go until tomorrow morning," she said wearily. "I will surely be glad when you're all healed up, and we don't have to go through this every day."

Peaches nickered and pushed her nose into Tory's chest. "I know, I know. You'll be glad, too." Tory laughed. "This hasn't exactly been a picnic for you, has it? I sure wish we knew what you did to injure that leg. We haven't been able to find a clue."

She gathered up the soiled dressings and stuffed them into a garbage bag she'd carried down just for that purpose. As she turned to head for the house, she heard a car coming over the hill. She watched as Robyn's tan Mazda headed down her driveway. She'd almost forgotten that it was Friday night, her regular Bible study night with her friend.

"Hey, am I in time to help?" Robyn's dark eyes sparkled with excitement as she jumped out of the car. "I've never had a horse for a patient. It'll look great on my résumé."

Tory made a face. "Sorry, Florence Nightingale. You're too late. The dirty work is already done." She tossed the bag of soiled dressings into a big metal trash can on the porch. "But come and say hello to Mocha Mix. You won't believe how much he's grown just since last week."

As soon as he saw the girls enter the barn, Mocha Mix pushed his moist nose up against the slats in his stall door, mooing mournfully. Robyn poked her fingers through the space between the boards and let the calf suck on her fingers. She giggled as he tried to pull her hand farther through the slats. "He has grown. And he's gotten stronger, too." She smiled up at Tory. "You're so lucky to have animals like these for friends."

"They're more like my kids," Tory said, wrinkling her nose. "Not that I think it's a bad thing to have kids. I just feel like I'm a little young to have a family." She laughed. "Especially a furry four-footed one."

Robyn pulled her hand from Mocha Mix's mouth. "Ah, you love every minute of it and you know it." Standing, she brushed the dirt from her knees. "Speaking of friends, what has become of the two-legged one with the blue eyes since I last talked to you? Any word from him?"

Tory shook her head. "Not a peep. I saw him in the hall earlier in the week, but he was walking the other way and didn't notice me."

"So-o-o, what happened? Why the sudden distance? Wasn't he on your doorstep every time you turned around? And now he's pretending you don't even exist." Robyn rolled her eyes in mock disgust. "Guys. Can't live with 'em and can't shoot 'em."

Tory laughed. "Kane is a nice guy. We've had some fun times together." She paused, wondering how much of her last conversation with Kane to reveal to Robyn. "We just ran into some spiritual incompatibilities. He's not a Christian, and I don't think he's comfortable with some of my beliefs. I'm not really surprised I haven't heard from him."

"Oh. That's different," Robyn said, suddenly serious. "I was just reading in my devotional book this morning about not being 'unequally yoked' with unbelievers. Something about light and darkness not mixing. But Kane doesn't seem 'dark.' He's so much fun to be around, and he's always laughing."

Tory nodded. "I know. I really like him. And I don't think it's fair to label anyone. That seems judgmental.

But I don't think the light and darkness part is describing people anyway. I think its talking about truth versus misinformation. I really believe that Kane misunderstands God. I wish I could figure out a way to explain it all to him."

"You know the old saying, 'You can lead a horse to water, but you can't make him drink,'" Robyn said. She gave Mocha Mix one last pat on the nose as the girls turned to walk toward the house. "What if Kane doesn't want to change how he views God?"

Tory shrugged. "I don't know. I don't see why we couldn't be friends, though. That is, if he still wants to be."

Just then a white truck appeared over the hill and bounced down Tory's driveway. Robyn gave her a sidelong glance. "Well," she said, a teasing tone in her voice, "I think we've just been given a clue that maybe he wants to be."

As Kane climbed out of the truck, Tory could see that he was carrying a huge bouquet of salmon colored roses. She heard Robyn gasp at the sight of the flowers.

"I believe we have a serious problem here," Robyn murmured, keeping her voice low enough that Kane couldn't hear her. "This is not 'just friends' behavior. I think I need to go home and leave you to deal with this."

"No!" Tory grabbed her friend's arm. "We have a study to do tonight. I'm not canceling it just . . . just because some guy shows up with the most gorgeous flowers I've ever seen."

Robyn gently pulled herself free and headed for her car. "Hi, Kane," she said as she passed him to get to her car. "Nice flowers. I'll see you later."

"You don't have to leave just because of me," he protested.

Robyn shook her head. "I've been here a while and had better get home." As she got into her car, she gave Tory a long look. Then she tooted her horn and drove away.

"What was that all about?" Kane watched Robyn's car disappear over the hill, a puzzled expression on his face. "Did I do something wrong? She acts as if she can't wait to get away from me." He pulled his shirt up and sniffed it. "Do I smell bad?"

Tory laughed. "I can't smell you." She pointed to the roses. "But I do smell those. They're beautiful."

"Oh, I forgot," Kane said, blushing. He handed the flowers to Tory. "These are yours. The color reminded me of you."

Tory held the roses and sank her face into the blooms, breathing deeply. "Thank you, Kane," she whispered. The delicate fragrance filled her nose and almost made her dizzy with its sweetness.

"Is there somewhere we could go to talk?" he asked. His voice had a serious tone, and his eyes had lost their twinkle.

"Sure," Tory said. She held the flowers up. "Let me put these in the house, and we can go for a walk. I have a secret place I go when I need to be alone to think. I'll take you there."

She hurried into the house and set the roses in the middle of the kitchen table. Their soft, glowing color seemed to light up the room. Mrs. Butler turned from the sink and gasped when she saw the bouquet.

"What gorgeous roses!" She dropped the potato she had been peeling and leaned over the table to sniff the largest bloom. "Isn't Kane coming in?" She straightened and peered around Tory and out into the yard.

Tory shook her head. "We have some talking to do and are going for a walk."

"Oh," her mother said, giving her a knowing glance. "Sounds serious." She slipped her arm around Tory's waist. "I'll be praying for you."

"I need it." Tory sighed heavily. "This is a tough one. I like Kane a lot. Why does life have to be so complicated sometimes?"

Mrs. Butler gave her daughter a squeeze. "I don't know. It's just the way it is, I guess. Wouldn't it be nice to have something like what the Israelite priests had back in Bible times during the days of the sanctuary? What were those stones called that they wore on the front of their robes?"

"The Urim and the Thummim, I think. I remember that from Bible class in sixth grade. Didn't they light up when the priests asked them questions to tell them what God wanted them to do? It would be great to have something like that now, to know for sure what God's will was in any given situation." She groaned. "Especially this one."

Dee Butler nodded sympathetically. "I've sure had times when I wished for the very same thing. At first I thought it didn't seem fair that back then they had such a direct line to God and such obvious answers when they asked for guidance. Then, when I thought about it some more, I realized that they didn't have the Bible back then the way we do. A lot of the guidance God gives us now is through His Word." She smiled at Tory. "We have all the information we need to discover God's will for us. But we just might have to dig a little to find it. And pray for wisdom."

"Well, I'm definitely doing that," Tory replied. She turned toward the door. "I'd better not keep Kane waiting any longer." She looked back at her mother standing there by the kitchen table, a look of concern on her face. "Thanks, Mom," she said. "It helped a lot to talk."

Mrs. Butler chuckled. "No extra charge. It's in my job description."

CHAPTER NINE

Kane followed Tory quietly as she led him down a narrow, winding path heading away from the gravel road. The little path broke out into a small clearing beside a stream. A large rock protruded out over the stream just below a miniature waterfall that tumbled into a crystal clear pool.

"Wow," Kane said, whistling in surprise. "This is incredible. No wonder you come here to think."

Tory sat down on the rock and scooted over to make room for Kane. She patted the place beside her, inviting him to sit down. "It is beautiful, isn't it? There's something soothing about the sound of water. Sometimes when life is really stressful, it feels as if my thoughts and feelings are a jumbled mass inside me. I can't even find an end to pull on to straighten them out. The peaceful sound of the water feels like gentle fingers, softly combing out my tangled thoughts so I can make sense of life again."

Kane nodded. "That makes a lot of sense. I like your analogy."

"Thanks. It works for me."

"Are you feeling stressed out by my being here?" he asked, tossing a pebble into the water. "Is that why you brought me here?"

She felt her face grow warm with embarrassment under his steady gaze. Looking away, she didn't answer for a long time, wondering how to tell him what was on her mind. "Yes, I guess so," she said, finally. "We need to talk, but everything seems so confusing."

"Are you upset that I brought you the roses?" he said softly.

"No. They're beautiful. I love them."

"Then what is it?"

Tory pulled her knees up close to her chin and wrapped her arms around her legs, rocking gently back and forth as she listened to the musical flow of the water over the rocks in the creek below her. A squirrel chattered in an old oak tree on the other side of the stream. She thought of Brian and how she had put him off when he wanted to have a relationship with her. Now it was too late for her to change her mind. He was in love with someone else. Had she made a terrible mistake in being so unsure of what she wanted? Was she making the same mistake now with Kane?

Father, help me, she cried inside, *I don't know what to do. Give me the words to say to Kane. Show me Your will.*

Kane reached over and took her hand. "I want to talk. I want to hear what you're thinking, how you're feeling. I want to tell you what I'm feeling. OK?"

"OK," she said, taking a deep breath. "But can I go first?"

He grinned. "Sure. Ladies first. I can live with that."

"First I need to tell you how much I think of you. How much fun it is to be with you. We've had some really great times together." Tory paused and took a deep breath. "If having fun and enjoying somebody's company was all there was to a relationship, there wouldn't be a problem. But since I've given my life to God, there's a lot more to it than that. His will has to come first instead of mine. You and I have different beliefs, different goals."

Frowning, Kane shook his head. "You make it sound like I'm a bad person that God doesn't want you to be around. I respect your beliefs. They're what makes you who you are. I would never try to change your mind in any way. So why can't we be together? I could learn a lot from you. Please don't shut me out. I'm not a bad person."

The pain in his eyes ripped at her heart. "I know you're not," she whispered. She squeezed his hand and stood up. "Let's go back to the house," she said, looking at the darkening woods around them. "We can talk about this more later, if that's all right with you."

Kane nodded and they walked back up the path to the road in silence.

Weeks passed and the weather grew colder. Kane came to the house often to take Tory flying or just to sit and talk. She didn't bring the subject of their relationship up again and noticed that he seemed to be carefully avoiding it, too. It was almost as if they both wanted to pretend the differences between them didn't exist.

The leaves on the old oak tree beside the waterfall in Tory's secret place turned bright yellow then fell to the ground, leaving the gnarled old trunk a stark silhouette against the gray sky of early winter. She came to the creek often. Although she missed the lushness of summer and the vivid colors of fall, she loved the crisp, cold air that signaled the arrival of winter.

Peaches' coat thickened with the icy winds that blew in from the north until she looked like a shaggy pony. Tory fed her in her stall now, letting her stay in the comfort of the barn for as long as she wanted to. Her leg had completely healed with only a jagged gray scar.

Mocha Mix no longer needed a bottle, so Tory turned him out into the pasture with Peaches. She fed both the mare and the calf extra hay and grain to help keep them warm through the long cold nights. Peaches' belly bulged so much that Tory couldn't imagine it being able to stretch any farther. Tory fervently wished she knew the exact time the mare had been bred so she could calculate the day she was due. As it was, she'd just have to watch her closely and hope the foal wouldn't be born out in the field.

As Christmas approached, Tory found herself having to spend more and more time studying for her nursing classes. Finals loomed just ahead and she knew she couldn't get any lower than a C grade in any of her classes and still remain in the program.

"Why did I think this was going to be easy?" she moaned to Robyn in the hall one day. "Sometimes I think my brain is going to fall right out of my head, I've been cramming so much information into it. Body systems, diseases of every description, drugs and biologicals . . . Isn't there a lethal level of studying that if you exceed it, you'll self-destruct?"

Robyn laughed. "Well, if there is, I think I've almost passed it." She shook her head. "I'm with you. I thought this two-year nursing course was going to be a breeze, but it's the hardest thing I've ever done. I saw a sweatshirt the other day with the question printed on it, 'Is there life after nursing school?' That pretty well sums up how I'm feeling right now."

"The part I like best is still clinical," Tory said. "I love getting to know the patients and feeling like I've done something to make them just a little more comfortable."

Robyn nodded in agreement. Then she brightened and turned to Tory with a questioning look. "Hey," she said, "whatever happened to Mr. Babcock? Since they moved me over to the other hospital for my clinical I haven't had a chance to drop in on him. Did his grand-daughter ever come to see him?"

Tory shook her head. "The nurse on his unit has been trying to reach her but so far has had no success. It seems as though the girl's mother is trying to block any efforts to contact her." She sighed. "He's such a lonely man. It's really sad. I watch him week by week losing weight and becoming weaker and weaker and wish we could do something to brighten up his life a lit-tle. He knows he's dying and has so little to live for."

"I know," Robyn said, excitement in her voice, "let's make him a Christmas care package. We could bake him some cookies and decorate a tiny tree to put up in his room."

Tory grabbed her friend's arm and swung her around in a circle. "Robyn, you are a genius. Let's do it right now. Do you have any more classes today?"

"No, I don't. We can go to the store to get the in-gredients, then take them to my house to bake them."

In less than an hour the girls were perched on stools in Robyn's kitchen, mixing flour, sugar, chocolate chips, and other ingredients together in a huge bowl. While the cookies baked, they cut tiny shapes from brightly colored foil and hung them on a miniature pot-ted pine tree.

"I'm glad we got him a living tree," Tory said as she hung a glittering yellow star on one of the branches. "He doesn't need another reminder that things die. I think it would be too depressing."

Robyn sat quietly, studying a piece of red foil in her

hands. Then she looked up at Tory with a look of confusion in her eyes. "You know, there's still a lot about death that I don't understand. I know how it happens from a clinical standpoint: someone's heart stops beating, their breathing ceases, and the brain cells die. But what happens then? My mom told me that the person goes straight to be with God in heaven, but I just read a verse the other day that said the dead are resurrected when Jesus comes back at the end of time. I'm not sure what to think."

"I've heard a lot of television preachers say that you go straight to heaven or hell when you die, too. That must be where your mom got it," Tory replied. "But that has never made sense to me. When Jesus raised Lazarus from the grave after he'd been dead for four days, he never said a word about his friend being in heaven. And if he'd gone to heaven where everything is perfect, why in the world would Jesus make him come back here?"

Robyn nodded as she shaped a tiny Christmas bell out of the red foil she was holding. "Yeah. That sounds pretty cruel to me. And speaking of cruel, the other thing that seems totally horrible to me is the idea that God would burn people constantly forever and ever if they didn't accept Jesus as their Saviour."

"That would make God the ultimate terrorist, wouldn't it?" Tory said, shuddering at the thought. "How could anyone serve Him out of love if their only other option was to be barbecued for eternity?"

"So, what is hell? And what happens to a person when they die?" Robyn hung her ornament on the tree and walked into the family room to get a Bible from the bookcase. She sat back down on the stool. "Show me where to find the answers, Tory," she said, handing her the Bible.

Her mind racing, trying desperately to remember some of the verses she'd read when studying about death, Tory flipped to the back of the Bible. She breathed a sigh of relief when she saw that it had a concordance that would help her find the places that mentioned death and hell.

"Get a pencil and paper, Robyn," she said. "Here's a whole list of verses about death and also about hell. Let's write them down, then we can look them up and compare them to see what the overall teaching of the Bible is on the subject."

Robyn grabbed a pencil from a jar on the kitchen counter and turned an old grocery store receipt over to write the list. "OK. Ready."

"First one is John 11:11-14. It looks like that's the one where Jesus said Lazarus was 'sleeping' when he died. And here is Ecclesiastes 9:5 and 6 that tells us that the dead don't know anything. 1 Corinthians 15:22, 23 is a good one. It says we'll be made alive at Christ's coming if we die. And here in John 6:40 and 44 it declares that Jesus will raise the dead that sleep in Him at the 'last day.' Psalm 115:17 talks about the dead going down to the grave in silence and not praising God. Doesn't sound to me like they're in heaven. There are lots more, too. Do you want all of them?"

Robyn shook her head. "Let me look up these first. It sounds pretty clear, but I want to study it out for myself. I like to read the verses before and after each one to get the setting and make sure I'm not misunderstanding what the writer is trying to say."

"That's a good idea." Tory laughed. "I heard someone say once that if you were going to establish a whole belief system based on sentences pulled from different places in the Bible, you could use the verse that says 'Judas went out and hung himself' and put it with the one in another part of the Bible that says 'Go thou and do likewise' and have a Biblical command to commit suicide!"

"What about hell. Are there any verses listed that talk about that?" Robyn leaned forward on her stool, nearly toppling it over. The aroma of cookies filled the kitchen.

Tory motioned toward the oven. "There are a bunch of them. But maybe we should take the cookies out of the oven before they burn." She set the Bible on the counter and reached for the hot pads. Soon racks of lightly-browned chocolate chip cookies lined the counter top.

"OK. Where were we," she mumbled under her breath as she picked the Bible back up and started leafing through the concordance section again. "All right, here are some verses. Are you ready, scribe?"

"Ready!" Robyn sat with pencil poised, waiting for the first text.

"Here's one that refers to eternal punishment. It's Matthew 25:46. Then one that records what the punishment of the wicked will be. That's Roman's 6:23 where it says the wages of sin is death. Psalm 37:20 describes the wicked vanishing like smoke. Second Thessalonians 1:6-11 says the wicked will be punished with everlasting destruction. Malachi 4:1-3 looks like a good one. It very clearly talks about the wicked being burned up 'root and branch' at the end of time."

Robyn stopped writing and sat thoughtfully. "So Jesus gives the people who follow Him everlasting life when He comes back at the end of time. And those who choose not to follow Him and cling to sin will get burned up then. That means no one is in heaven or in hell now, but dying is like going to sleep until Jesus comes."

"Sounds that way to me," Tory said. "But I'd study

it out some more. Look them all up." She pointed to the back of Robyn's Bible. "It's easy to find them when you use this concordance. And here's a list of the meanings of the word 'hell' when it's used in the Bible. This is pretty fascinating stuff. According to this, the word 'Hades' that is translated 'hell' is really 'the grave' or 'the abode of the dead.'"

Robyn took the Bible and placed it back on the shelf. She smiled at Tory. "I've learned a lot since we started studying together. But I can see I still have a lot more to do. I like it, though. It's as if the lights are coming on and I can see spiritual things more and more clearly. And it's a great feeling." She pulled a cookie tin from the cupboard. "Right now we'd better get these cookies packaged up and take them to Mr. Babcock."

"Agreed," Tory said, stacking cookies in neat little piles. "I can't wait to see his face when we walk in the room with these."

CHAPTER TEN

A feeling of Christmas filled the air as the girls hurried through the hospital lobby with their gifts. Gold and silver garlands draped the halls on the way to Mr. Babcock's room, and a huge holly wreath hung on the wall next to the nurse's station. Several nurses turned to admire the miniature Christmas tree that Tory carried in her arms.

As they reached Mr. Babcock's room, she stopped short. The door was shut tight. She knew that her patient never closed his door unless he was feeling very ill and wanted no visitors.

"What is it?" Robyn whispered. "Do you think he's too sick to see us?"

Tory shook her head. "I don't know."

Just then the door opened slightly and a beautiful young woman with long dark hair slipped out, almost bumping into Tory.

"Oh, excuse me," the girl said, then burst into tears. Tory stared as she recognized the girl's round face from the picture on Mr. Babcock's bedside stand.

"You're Mr. Babcock's granddaughter!"

It was the girl's turn to stare. She looked at the little Christmas tree that Tory held and at the tin of cookies in Robyn's hands. "How do you know who I am?" she asked, sniffling. "And what are you doing here?"

"I'm your grandfather's student nurse," Tory replied quickly, "and he told me all about you. He wanted to see you so badly, I'm sure he must be thrilled to see you." She held out the little Christmas tree. "Here. We decorated this tree for him to cheer him up because he missed you so much, but now that you're here, I'm sure he doesn't need any more cheering up."

The girl burst into tears again, covering her face with her hands and sobbing as if her heart would break. "It's too late," she moaned. "Grandpa is dead. I didn't even get to say goodbye." Sinking down onto the floor, she leaned against the door frame to her grandfather's room. Tory sat down beside her. Putting her arm around the girl's shoulder, she held her while she cried. Robyn stood, holding the tin of cookies, a helpless look on her face.

One of the staff nurses noticed the girls in the hallway and hurried toward them. She gently lifted the heartbroken girl to her feet, leading her to a more private place where she could grieve.

Tory watched the girl shuffle out of sight. Tears welled up in her eyes as she thought of Mr. Babcock and how he had missed seeing his beloved granddaughter by just a few minutes. She had come to love him, too, in the months that she'd been his nurse.

Robyn reached over and gave her a hug. "This is the hard part of being a nurse," she said, her voice heavy. "What should we do with the tree and the cookies?"

"I think we should leave them for Mr. Babcock's granddaughter," Tory answered. "Maybe having something made especially for her grandfather will be of some comfort to her."

Robyn nodded in agreement and pulled a pen and a pad of paper from her backpack. "Here's something to write a note on."

Tory wrote her address and phone number on a piece of the paper and jotted a short note explaining why she and Robyn had left the tree and cookies for her. "Please call me," she said. "I know you must wonder about your grandfather's last days. I would love to share with you some of the memories I have of him." She signed her name and stuck the note with the cookie tin and tree.

The tall slender nurse that Tory had first talked to about Mr. Babcock's desire to see his granddaughter was sitting behind the nurse's station as the girls approached. Tory handed her the tree and the tin.

"Could you please see that Mr. Babcock's granddaughter gets these?" she asked.

The nurse smiled sadly. "I sure will," she said. "Isn't it too bad that he didn't get to see her?"

Tory nodded. "Thanks for contacting her anyway. And for passing these along to her."

"No problem."

An icy rain started to fall as the girls made their way back across the parking lot to Robyn's car. The gray sodden sky looked as overcast as Tory's heart felt. She turned to Robyn as she slipped into the passenger seat of the car.

"You know, sometimes things just don't turn out very well, do they?"

As she thought of the heartache that Mr. Babcock's granddaughter must be feeling, all of her own losses came rolling back like a thick blanket of fog, smothering her with sadness.

It was almost dark when Tory arrived home that night. Even the sight of the Christmas tree in the front window failed to lift her spirits. Ordinarily she loved Christmas with all its bright color and tradition, but tonight her heart felt too heavy to celebrate. She parked her car in the driveway and headed down to check on Peaches without even saying hello to her parents.

The mare nickered a greeting from the stall, then began moving restlessly back and forth as if looking for something she'd lost. Tory slipped into the stall and ran her hand along the underside of the mare's belly. It was tight as a drum and sweat covered her flanks. The animal repeatedly turned her head to look back at her abdomen as if she didn't understand why it was hurting so much. When Tory reached up underneath her and felt her milk bag, she discovered that the teats were covered with a waxy coating and dripping thin, blue milk.

"Peaches," Tory exclaimed, "you're having your baby now, aren't you!"

Suddenly nervous, she checked the mare's water and then grabbed a shovel and mucked out the stall. She didn't want any manure to contaminate the foaling area. Breaking open a bale of fresh straw, she scattered it generously over the floor of the stall.

"I'll leave you alone for a while, girl," she said when she'd done everything she could think of to make the stall safe and comfortable. She scratched Peaches behind the ears. "I need to go up and get something to eat, but I'll be back soon to check on you."

As soon as she had finished her supper, Tory went straight back to the barn to see how the mare's labor was progressing. Peaches alternated lying down and standing up. When she was up, she nosed in her water bucket but made no attempt to drink.

The sun had long since set and the stall was as dark as a cave. Tory hung a lantern from a hook near the door of the stall and lit it. She knew Peaches didn't need the light, but she wanted to be able to see everything that was going on with the horse.

For hours Tory sat in the corner of the stall, trying to stay out of the mare's way but observing her progress. Several times Mr. Butler came out to check on her, once to bring her a blanket and pillow and another time a thermos of hot herb tea.

"Thanks, Dad," Tory said gratefully as she poured the steaming beverage into an insulated cup. "It is cold out here. This will help warm me up."

As time went by, Peaches began to get more restless. Again and again she lay down only to get right back up. Her breath came in steaming snorts, the moisture freezing midair like a miniature cloud under her muzzle. Tory watched her, puzzled. Why wasn't the foal coming? Something didn't seem right.

Then, as Peaches swung around in the stall, Tory saw two little black hooves protruding from the birth canal. The next time the mare lay back down, she edged in for a closer look. She knew that foals could only be born one way—with the front hooves tucked up under the nose so the head and front feet would come out together. If the foal's head was down and wedged, it would die.

"Easy, girl, easy," Tory said, trying to calm the mare while her own thoughts raced like a herd of wild horses. Just then her father's face appeared in the opening over the stall door. He held a granola bar and an apple in his hand.

"Just thought you might be getting hungry," he said. His smile faded as he saw Tory's face. "What is it? Is she having trouble?"

"I'm afraid the foal is wedged," Tory explained, her voice tight with fear. "I should have realized it before now. Things just weren't moving as fast as they should have, but it didn't even dawn on me that the foal wasn't coming right until I saw that." She pointed to the little feet protruding from the mare's body. "It's too late to call the vet. She lives so far away, she'd never get here in time. The baby would be dead and Peaches might be, too." She looked pleadingly at her father. "I know you've turned calves before. Will you help me reposition the foal?"

Mr. Butler rubbed his chin thoughtfully. "Well, I guess we can give it a try. I've never dealt with horses much. They aren't exactly like cows. Seem more temperamental and fragile."

"We *have* to do it, Dad." She wiped away the tears that were starting to trickle down her cheeks. It was no time to let her emotions distract her. "Tell me what to do first."

Following her father's instructions, she prepared an antiseptic solution and scrubbed her hands and arms almost to her armpits. She set some of the solution aside to use on the little one's umbilical cord after it was born. Mr. Butler held Peaches' head while Tory plunged both of her arms into the birth canal, pushing the foal back and releasing his wedged head with one smooth movement. The little body felt limp and lifeless to her touch.

Please, God, let him live.

Once Tory had the foal repositioned, Peaches gave several heaving pushes. The little one slid right out of the birth canal and onto the straw. The mare lay quietly for a few minutes, making no attempt to stand up. Tory cleared the remnants of the birthing bag from the foal's face and nostrils. She stood beside him, barely daring to breathe, waiting for some movement, some sign of life in the tiny body. Mr. Butler watched silently beside her. When one of the foal's tiny feet jerked just a little, she heard her father draw in a sharp breath. She knew he had been wondering, too, if the little one would live.

Peaches stood up, snapping the umbilical cord that had connected her to her baby. Then she turned and began licking the foal vigorously from head to foot.

"Dad, just look at him," Tory squealed in delight. "He's jet black. There's not one white mark anywhere on his body. He looks like a little poppyseed beside his huge mom."

"Poppyseed, huh?" Mr. Butler chuckled. "Sounds like you've come up with a name for the little guy already. Although his name should be Lucky or Downright Fortunate. It's a wonder he survived what he just went through." He turned to leave. "I'm going up to the house," he said, wearily. "This maternity stuff is exhausting. I'm sure you'll want to stay until you make sure the little geezer can nurse and go to the bathroom. Can you handle that part without me?"

Tory hugged her dad. "Sure. I'll be up after awhile." She sighed with relief and sank down into the straw, pulling the blanket up around her shoulders. The foal shuddered, opened its eyes, and tried to stand up. Tory slipped quickly to his side and gently held him down. Carefully, she applied the antiseptic solution to the stump of his umbilical cord. She grabbed a clean towel that she had hung close by and briskly rubbed the foals damp coat until he was completely dry.

"Well, here goes, little guy," she said as she tossed the soiled towel aside. "It's time to get down to business."

A feeling of excitement welled up within her. She had been studying the training journals for months. The most up-to-date information on foal training focused on the work to be done with a foal during the few minutes right after birth when it imprinted to its mother and to any other nearby creature. She knew that this tendency of the foal to imprint was a survival technique, designed by God to create a desire in the baby to stay close to and obey the older, more experienced members of the herd. "Just consider me your Aunt Tory," she whispered to the foal. "I'm going to teach you some things that your horsey relatives wouldn't even dream of."

CHAPTER
ELEVEN

Peaches nickered and nosed her baby as Tory held Poppyseed down, keeping the little fellow from struggling to his feet.

"It's all right, Mama," she said, reaching up to stroke the mare's soft muzzle. "The things I'm going to teach this guy are going to make him a great horse later."

She positioned herself on her knees in the straw just behind Poppyseed's shoulders, gently but firmly keeping him on his side. It seemed cruel to hold the foal against his will, but she knew that because a horse's main defense when threatened is to run away, holding the foal down during the period of imprinting would create an attitude of submission to humans that would last the rest of his life.

Starting with Poppyseed's head, Tory began to rub the foal's body with her fingertips. "They call this desentization," she whispered. "When you get used to all this handling now, it won't bother you at all when you're older."

At first, the foal resisted, trying to pull away from her moving fingers. Tory worked with each area until he relaxed and no longer reacted to her touch. She rubbed all around his muzzle, into his ears, around his eyes, and stuck her fingers into his mouth, massaging his upper lip and rubbing all over on his tongue.

"There. You won't ever fight having a bit put in your mouth now." She worked her way down his neck and over his little crest. When she moved down one of his forelegs, he jerked back and began to struggle again to get up. Peaches moved restlessly in the stall, clearly worried about the treatment her infant was receiving.

"It's going to be OK, Peaches. I'm not going to hurt him, I promise." She held the foal down, murmuring nonsense to him until he quieted. Then she took his tiny hoof in her hand and began softly slapping the bottom 50 times in a soft rhythmic motion. "This is to get you used to having horseshoes put on and your feet handled."

As she rubbed the area around the foal's chest and abdomen, Tory avoided the spot on his side where eventually the rider's heel would touch. In later training sessions she would be teaching Poppyseed to respond to pressure in that area, and she didn't want him to be desensitized to it. She worked with each of his legs, flexing each joint again and again until they moved freely and without resistance.

The whole procedure took less than an hour. As soon as she was finished, Tory released the foal and scooted back in the straw to watch what he would do. Peaches licked his face and nudged him, encouraging him to get up. With a burst of effort, Poppyseed struggled to his feet and stood on wobbly legs. He nuzzled his mother and searched along her flank for her udder.

Tory smiled as the foal found the right spot and began to nurse, his stubby little tail twitching madly. "I can see that you're going to be just fine," she said, patting the little fellow gently on the rump. Yawning and stretching, she suddenly realized how tired she was. Standing, she turned out the lantern. "Good night, you guys. I'm going to bed."

Early the next morning Tory was back down at the barn. She didn't want too much time to go by between the first and second sessions of imprint training. All the training manuals stressed the importance of reinforcing lessons right away while the foal was still in its first few hours of life.

Peaches stood munching hay when Tory peeked into the stall. Poppyseed lay in the straw, stretched out and relaxed, looking like a dark little shadow in the dim light of the stall.

"How is my favorite horse family?" Tory said cheerfully. She slipped into the stall and moved smoothly to Poppyseed's side. This time he didn't resist as she held him down and repeated last night's procedure. When she had finished, she allowed the foal to stand up. Using the flat of her hand, she pressed the saddle area on his back just hard enough so that he felt the weight. She repeated the motion over and over. Then she encircled the girth area with her arms and clasped her hands under the foal's chest. Rhythmically and repetitiously, she squeezed him about 50 times.

"You won't even consider bucking when a saddle is cinched down on you now, little one," she cooed. Then she ran her hands down his legs and picked up each of his hooves, tapping the soles as she had done the first time. The foal never flinched, but let her manipulate his feet and legs any way she wanted to.

When she had finished, she stepped back. Poppyseed ran to his mother's side, but before he nursed he turned to look at Tory, an expression of curiosity in his dark eyes. Tory was amazed at the change in the foal in just a few hours. His coal-black coat appeared more fluffy than it had right after birth, and he was much more steady on his feet.

"You did good work, Peaches," she said, pulling a handful of grain from the bag just outside the stall door and offering it to the mare. "You have the world's most beautiful baby."

It was hard for Tory to keep her eyes open in classes after being up most of the night attending Poppyseed's birth. She couldn't wait to see Robyn to tell her about the new foal. Finally, during lunch break, she saw her friend across the cafeteria. She waved and mouthed the words, "I have something to tell you."

"I have something to tell you, too," Robyn mouthed back.

Hurriedly finishing up the last few bites of her salad, Tory put away her tray and joined her friend.

"So, what's your news?" Robyn asked. "Come on, spill it. No, let me guess. You're flying to Tahiti with the blue-eyed wonder."

Tory rolled her eyes. "No. Why would you ever say that? It's even better than that."

"What could be better than Tahiti?" Robyn grinned. "Unless of course one is viewing the world through horse-colored glasses. Then, I guess a ranch in Montana or Oregon with horse trails meandering over mountain passes would be more appealing."

Tory groaned. "Earth to Robyn. I'm talking reality here. Peaches had her foal last night. He's jet black and cute as he can be. I stayed up most of the night helping with the birth and then doing imprint training on him."

"What?" Robyn's mouth dropped open in surprise. "You started training the poor little thing before he was even a day old?"

"Before he was even an hour old." Tory smiled at the memory. "It was amazing. Now he'll be much eas-ier to train as he gets older. What he learns the first few hours after he's born will stay with him permanently."

Robyn shook her head. "It's news to me. But I believe you. I wish I knew even half of what you do about horses. I'm hoping I'll get a chance to learn. I'd love to have a horse of my own."

"Well, you're welcome to help me with Poppyseed and to ride Peaches any time you want to," Tory said. She looked at her friend quizzically. "Now, what is your news?"

Robyn smiled mysteriously. "My news has something to do with being born, too, only not physically."

"What are you talking about?" Tory frowned, trying to make sense of her words. "How else can something be born?"

"Think about it," Robyn said. "Do you remember our last Bible study? What topic were we researching?"

"Baptism," Tory said. "What about it?"

Robyn's face seemed to light up with an excitement Tory had never seen in her before. "I've made a decision to do it," she said. "I've been dancing around the edges of this Christianity stuff long enough. The Bible makes it very clear that Jesus is God and that the only way to find true peace of heart is to make a decision to follow Him. The more we've studied together, the more convinced I've become that this is what I want for my life, whatever it takes. It's so different from anything I've ever done before, and I feel so different; it's like being born all over again, but into a whole, new world."

Tory grabbed her friend and gave her a big hug. "That is such incredible news. Much more exciting than mine. When are you thinking about being baptized?"

"I'd like to do it on New Year's Day. It's on a Friday this year," Robyn said. "Doesn't that seem perfect, starting a new life on the first day of a new year?" She frowned. "The only problem is my mom. She hasn't been all that thrilled about our studying together. Every time I bring up something that we've been studying, she gets an annoyed look on her face and changes the subject. She really acted funny when I started going to church with you. I don't know what she'll think about my decision to get baptized."

Tory took her friend's sleeve and pulled her outside onto the lawn. A gust of cold wind blew down through the campus, and both girls shivered and turned the collars of their coats up to protect their necks from the icy blast.

"Let's pray right now for your mom," Tory suggested.

Robyn glanced around at the big plate glass window behind them. "Don't look now," she said, with a nervous giggle, "but she's watching us as we speak. Do you think she suspects we're talking about her?"

"Here," Tory said, looping her arm through Robyn's. "I'll walk you to your car. That way she won't suspect a thing."

As the girls went along, they each prayed for Mrs. Thompson, asking that God would open her heart so she would want to listen to the things Robyn longed to share with her.

"You know," Robyn said after they had finished praying, "I think my mom is mad at God. She never really was what you'd call religious, although she let me go to church with friends when I was little, and I have seen her read the Bible." She reached down and picked up a small stone from beside the sidewalk and tucked it into her pocket. "But that was before Dad left. He took off with another woman. Since he's been gone, she's seemed angry a lot of the time. At first I thought she was mad at me, but after a while I realized that she was angry at life."

Tory's heart ached for her friend as she saw the pain in her eyes. "I'm sorry, Robyn. I didn't know. I guess I never really thought about you and your mom living together alone. I didn't realize your dad wasn't there with you until just recently."

"Yeah." Robyn made a face. "It's been the pits. And it seems like my finding something so meaningful in my life has just made Mom hurt more. Does that make sense?"

Tory nodded. "A lot of sense."

"But I have to do what's right for me," Robyn said with a sigh. She pulled her keys from her pocket and unlocked the door of her car. "And this decision is right for me. I just wish Mom understood."

As Tory watched her friend drive away, she swallowed hard. *Father, why does life have to be so full of hard choices? Please go with Robyn and give her the wisdom and courage to do what she needs to do.*

CHAPTER TWELVE

Tory stretched and yawned, ready to get up and start another busy day. Then she remembered. It was Christmas break and classes wouldn't start again until the first week in January! Jumping out of bed, she ran to the window. A light dusting of snow lay on the ground. It covered the roof of the barn like sugar coating on a gingerbread house.

Peaches stood in the paddock, Poppyseed at her side. The little fellow was much more steady on his long spindly legs than he had been only days before. Tory giggled as she watched him stretch down, trying to sniff the snow that lay at his feet. When his nose touched the cold, wet stuff, he jerked back with a snort of surprise. Peaches nuzzled him as if to reassure him that snow was a normal part of life and he had no need to fear it. The foal pressed close to his mother's side, nibbling at her shoulder.

"You little corker," Tory said, shaking her head. "You're already showing signs of serious mischievousness. What will you be like when you're older?"

As if he could hear her words, the foal darted from his mother's side and kicked up his little heels, sending himself toppling headfirst into the snow. Tory laughed until her sides ached. As she doubled over with laughter, she heard a knock on her bedroom door.

"C-come in," she called, hiccuping.

Dee Butler poked her head in the door. "What in the world is going on in here?" She walked over to the window and looked out. Poppyseed was just staggering to his feet, his dark little face powdered with snow.

"What a little imp he is!" Mrs. Butler said, chuckling. "Are you sure you don't want to call him Diablo instead of Poppyseed?"

Tory shook her head, wiping her eyes. "I'm sure," she said. "I don't want to label him as something bad. He's too sweet."

"When are you going to start training him to lead?"

Pulling a soft cotton rope and a tiny halter from one of her dresser drawers, Tory held them up for her mother to see. "Right now," she said.

"Do you mean right now 'right now' or after breakfast 'right now'?" Mrs. Butler asked, raising her eyebrows questioningly. "I made biscuits and honey for you since this is the first day of your Christmas break. They'll be cold and hard if you don't eat them pretty soon."

Tory tossed the rope and halter on her bed. "Well, in that case, I definitely mean after breakfast 'right now.'"

The thin rays of the winter sun were already melting the snow as Tory pulled on her rubber barn boots and wiggled into her down coat. She grabbed the halter and rope and headed for the paddock. Poppyseed showed no sign of fear as she approached. He followed Peaches as she pushed her way up to the fence to get a treat, then sidled around her to sniff Tory's outstretched hand with curiosity and friendly trust.

"It's time for your next lesson," she said softly, reaching out to touch the foal's soft coat. Pulling the rope from her pocket, she let Poppyseed smell it. Then she let him sniff the halter. He stood obediently as she briefly repeated all the desensitizing steps she had taken in his first two training sessions, rubbing his head, body, and legs, and picking up each foot to tap it gently on the sole.

When she slipped the halter on over his muzzle and ears and fastened the throatlatch under his furry little chin, he tensed for a moment. Tory paused, talking to him in soft, smooth tones until he relaxed again. She moved to his side, making sure he was facing his mother, and gently tugged on the halter, pulling him sideways toward Peaches. As soon as the foal took one step, in an attempt to keep his balance, she immediately rewarded him by releasing the pressure on his halter. Before long, Poppyseed walked behind Tory in response to her gentle coaxing.

"OK, guy," she said finally. "Enough for one day." She kissed him on his furry forehead. "You are a star pupil."

"And I see a star teacher at work, too," Tory heard a voice say from the top of the board railing behind her. She turned to see Kane sitting there, a smile on his face and a sprig of mistletoe tied with a red ribbon in his hand.

"I didn't even hear you drive up. How long have you been watching me?" Tory blushed to think of someone listening to her conversation with the foal. She tried to remember if she'd said anything really embarrassing.

Kane jumped down from the fence, but kept a comfortable distance from Poppyseed. Tory could see he was making an effort not to scare the foal, and she appreciated his sensitivity to the situation. "I haven't been here very long," he confessed. "Just long enough to see you teach that little booger to lead. Pretty impressive stuff. I'd never have thought a horse so young could learn so much. Guess I underestimated the critters."

Tory unbuckled the halter and slid it off over Poppyseed's ears. "A lot of people do," she said, chuckling as the foal ran to his mother's side, kicking up his heels and tossing his head. "This is actually the ideal time to begin his training. It's just like they say about kids—that the first few years of their lives are the most important as far as laying the groundwork for the next 80. It's the same with horses, only its the first few hours, days, and weeks that make a difference."

"What are you going to teach him next?" Kane asked, an interested expression on his face.

Tory coiled the soft cotton rope she'd been using on Poppyseed and hung it with the halter on a fencepost. "I'm going to teach him to respond to heel pressure and leg pressure. I'll do that by standing alongside him and reaching over his back, pressing the area on his side where later the rider's heel will press. As soon as he moves sideways toward me, I'll let up the pressure to reward him. Eventually, he'll automatically move sideways in response to leg aids."

"Wow," Kane said, shaking his head. "This is so amazing. What a lucky horse he is to have you for his human."

Tory gazed at the black foal, now nursing contentedly at Peaches' side. "I think I'm definitely the lucky one. He's a real gift to me."

"You mean a gift from your parents?"

"Well, that, too," Tory said. "But I meant a gift from God. A blessing. I've really learned a lot in working with him about how God might feel about me. How much He must want me to be happy and be the best I can be. There's a lot I don't understand about the way He works sometimes. But just like I know Poppyseed doesn't have a clue about why I'm doing some of the things I am with him, because there's no way he can see the future and what he'll need to know to be a well-trained saddle horse, so I know God has plans for me that I can't see now."

Kane stared at the mistletoe in his hands, a frown wrinkling his forehead as it had so many times before when Tory brought up anything about a personal relationship with God. But he said nothing.

"Hey, why don't you come on up to the house for some hot apple cider," Tory suggested. "I've been out here too long and could use something warm to thaw my bones."

Seemingly relieved at the change in the subject, he followed her out through the wooden gate. She retrieved the halter and lead rope from the post where she'd left them, making a quick detour into the barn to put them away. As she glanced back at Kane, she noticed him tucking the mistletoe into his jeans pocket.

"You know, I need to go," he said as she walked back out of the tack room. "I'd love to stay and have some cider, but I can't. I have some errands to run."

Tory nodded, swallowing the growing feeling that Kane was trying to come up with a reason to get away from her. "Sure. Thanks for dropping by. It was good to see you."

She watched him drive away and noticed that he didn't look back and wave as he left.

Christmas break passed by in a blur of activity, including Christmas shopping and continued training sessions with Poppyseed. Christmas morning found a brand-new set of matching halters for Peaches and Poppyseed under the tree. Tory had asked her parents to invite Robyn and her mother over for Christmas dinner, and now she waited excitedly for them to arrive. It was almost noon when the familiar tan Mazda pulled into the drive and Robyn jumped out, dressed in jeans and cowboy boots.

"She's bound and determined to ride a horse today," Mrs. Thompson said, laughing, as she got out of the car. "She said you told her it was OK to start riding Peaches again."

"Yep. That's what I told her," Tory replied, grinning at Robyn. "Are you ready to go now?" Robyn nodded vigorously and the two headed for the barn.

Peaches stood in the paddock and nickered at the girls as they approached. Tory ducked into the tack room and grabbed the mare's bridle, looped it over the horn of her saddle, and carried the whole thing out to the alley of the barn. She walked right up to Peaches and slipped the bridle's bit into her mouth, pulling the headstall up over her ears.

"Maternity leave is officially over, girl," she said. "Sorry about that."

As she led Peaches to the place where she always saddled her, she explained the procedure to Robyn. She showed her how to brush the mare down before saddling her, making sure the brush strokes always followed the direction the hair naturally grew. Letting Robyn toss the saddle blanket up into place, she explained how to place it higher than she wanted it to be, then pull it back down into place to make sure there were no hairs kinked in the wrong direction to cause the horse discomfort under the saddle.

Robyn's face turned red as she heaved the heavy saddle up on top of the saddle blanket. "Whew," she grunted. "That thing is heavier than it looks." She watched carefully as Tory showed her how to tighten the cinch and tie the special knot that held the saddle in place.

Before they climbed up into the saddle, Tory picked up each one of Peaches' hooves and checked for rocks and debris wedged between the horseshoe. "I can't afford to let some little rock make my horse lame," she said, tossing the hoof pick back into the bucket of grooming supplies. Finally she led the mare out into the barn lot.

"Let's ride double first," she said, glancing back toward the house. "Dinner will be a while, and it will give us a chance to talk." She swung up into the saddle and held a hand out to Robyn.

"Sounds good to me," Robyn replied. She grabbed Tory's hand as she slipped her left toe into the stirrup and vaulted up and onto the back of the saddle behind Tory. Peaches quivered slightly at the feel of two riders, then immediately calmed to her usual placid self.

The sky stretched over the fields, a clear robin's egg blue, and the sunlight glinted on the melting frost, making each spear of dead grass sparkle like a stalk of jewels. The girls followed a cow path through the creek and across the airstrip to the pond in which Mocha Mix's mother had died.

"Where is Mocha Mix?" Robyn asked. "I didn't see him in the barn lot."

Tory pointed to a herd of cattle grazing at the far end of the airstrip. A dark brown and white spotted calf watched them from the edge of the herd.

"Watch this," Tory said. She handed the reins to Robyn and slipped down out of the saddle. "Here, Mocha. Come here, boy," she called. The calf broke from the herd and started running toward them, bawling a greeting. Tory held her arms out and as the calf reached her, she dropped to her knees and hugged him. "You think I'm your mother, don't you?"

Robyn laughed as the calf licked Tory's face. "I don't think there's any doubt in his little bovine heart," she said with a chuckle.

Back in the saddle, Tory reined Peaches around to the farside of the pond. Tattered cattails thrust upward out of the ice at the edges of the water, weary sentinels standing guard over their frozen world.

"Br-r-r." Tory shivered. "That sunshine is deceptive. This is a winter day, for sure. Before we know it, it will be January.

Robyn beamed. "And I will be having my baptism."

"And how is your mother taking the news?" Tory asked, feeling a rush of concern for her friend.

Robyn shook her head. "She doesn't know yet," she said in a small voice.

CHAPTER THIRTEEN

January 1 dawned cold and still. Tory shivered as she climbed out of bed and pulled on a warm robe. Frost decorated her bedroom window with crystal ferns and delicate plumes of ice. She thought of Robyn's baptism that night and hoped that the baptistry in the church was warm.

Smiling to herself, she pictured Robyn's excitement over her baptism.

"It's more important to me than getting married," she had told Tory on the phone earlier in the week. "This is my chance to tell the world how much Jesus means to me."

"So, have you told your mother?" Tory had asked.

A long silence on the other end of the line. Then Robyn answered quietly, "Yes. I did."

"Well, what did she say?"

"She said she wouldn't come to the baptism with me."

Tory cringed as she remembered the pain in her friend's voice.

A Christmas wreath still hung on the front door of the church as Tory and her parents climbed the steps and entered at a few minutes before 7:00 that night. The sanctuary seemed to glow with a soft light as they found seats near the front where they had the best view of the baptistry. As they settled into their places, Tory glanced around her and realized that the soft glow came from scores of candles set in each window sill and in strategic places around the church.

One of the church musicians came forward and started playing praise songs on the keyboard. Beautiful nature scenes, most of them featuring waterfalls, rivers, or pictures of the ocean appeared from a video projected on the overhead screen.

"This is wonderful," Tory whispered to her mother. "I love the way they chose water scenes for this. It's perfect for a baptism."

Mrs. Butler nodded and smiled. "I'll bet Robyn planned this out herself. It's going to be really special. I can tell already."

A young woman Tory had seen at church but hadn't had a chance to meet yet, moved to the front, and in a clear soprano voice began to sing, "My Jesus, I Love Thee." Tory felt a lump growing in her throat as she listened to the words. She thought of Kane and felt an overwhelming longing for him to know Jesus as his Saviour. A feeling of sadness settled over her as she realized that he might never want to know Him or accept Him. That God honored his free choice and would never force him in a direction that he didn't want to go.

Oh, Father, she prayed, *this hurts too much. How much You must hurt over giving up even one of Your children that refuses to accept Your love.*

She tried to shake the melancholy thought and focus on the baptismal ceremony. *God's heart must be very happy right now,* she thought, *as all of heaven rejoices together over Robyn's decision to follow Jesus.* She looked around at the people gathered in the little church, searching for Mrs. Thompson's face. Hoping that she had changed her mind and decided to come and support her daughter. But she was nowhere to be seen.

A young man got up and shared with the group the story of his life before he surrendered it to God and how much it had changed when he did. Tory could see tears in the eyes of many of the people in the audience as they nodded in agreement with what he was saying. She remembered the boy when he had been heavily involved with drugs and alcohol. Seeing him around town, she had shuddered at the vacant look in his eyes and the anger and despair that had clung to him like a dark cloak. Now his face seemed to glow with happiness as he talked of the purpose Jesus had given his life.

As soon as the young man finished speaking, Pastor Don appeared in the baptistry, dressed in a blue robe. He looked out at the congregation and smiled broadly.

"It's a happy day," he said. "One of the happiest I've had for a long time. It's not often that I get the opportunity to do what I'm going to do tonight."

Tory looked around at the others in the crowd. They all had the same perplexed expression that she was sure must be on her own face. Hadn't Pastor Don performed many baptisms? Why was this one such a rare opportunity for him?

"Robyn Thompson has decided to be baptized today after months of studying with her friend, Tory Butler, and with me." He motioned for Tory to stand up, then reached up to help Robyn down into the baptistry. "But the story doesn't end there. Some time ago a woman came to my office here at the church with a question. She said she was a counselor at the college, and a certain student wouldn't take an exam on Saturday because of her belief in keeping the Sabbath holy and set apart for God. So she wanted to know more about the Sabbath, because she felt that if it was important enough to make a student willing to give up her nursing career plans to honor it, it must be important indeed."

Tory caught her breath as the pastor continued. "As we studied together, this woman shared with me the pain that she'd experienced in her life and how she felt it was impossible for her to forgive those who had hurt her, but she knew that bitterness was eating away her very soul and she longed to find peace of mind. Unbeknown to her daughter, she has been studying with me for months, and has found, in the pages of the Bible and in the heart of the God those pages reveal, the peace she was seeking."

The pastor reached his hand up again, and this time it was Mrs. Thompson who stepped into the baptistry to join her daughter. Tears streamed down Robyn's face as she threw her arms around her mother.

"So you see, folks," the pastor said, as he lifted his hands over the two women. "Miracles happen. We're witnessing one right here."

After the baptism, Robyn and Mrs. Thompson stood in the foyer of the church while the people filed by to hug and congratulate them. As Tory's turn came to greet them, she wasn't sure whether to laugh or cry.

"I can't believe this," she said, hugging both of them several times. "What an incredible day!"

Mrs. Thompson gave Robyn a sidelong glance and chuckled through her tears. "Yes," she said. "It will go down in the books as a red letter day, for sure."

"I've always heard it said that today is the first day of the rest of your life," Robyn said, her eyes shining with joy. "But this one feels more like the first day than any I've ever had before."

Months passed and the dull grays of winter gave

way to spring's bright pastels. Tory spent every spare minute after classes and clinicals working with Poppyseed. The days lengthened and warmed, and the colt's fuzzy winter coat thinned out to a slick, shiny black. As often as she could, Robyn joined Tory in the training sessions, helping her reinforce the lessons in backing, leading, loading into a horse trailer, and tolerating grooming procedures.

"Could I ride Peaches today?" Robyn pleaded one Sunday afternoon. "Around the barrels, I mean. The real thing."

Tory looked at her friend dubiously. "Are you sure you're ready for that?"

"As ready as I'll ever be," she answered, her voice quavering just enough for Tory to realize how nervous she really was.

"OK. But if you're ready to do the barrels, then you're ready to get her saddled up, too. You know where the tack room is."

Robyn gulped and nodded. "I can handle that," she said, heading for the tack room. Tory made it a point not to follow her, busying herself with setting the empty barrels up in the field beside the barn.

"E-e-e-k-k," came a shrill shriek from inside the tack room. Tory sprinted across the field and dived through the barbed wire fence, ripping the sleeve of her T-shirt as she went. As she burst into the tack room, expecting to find Robyn in mortal danger, she saw her friend backed into the far corner pointing at a huge spiderweb spun from the horn of Peaches' saddle to the hook where the bridle hung.

"I-It almost got me," Robyn stammered, a horrified expression on her face.

"What?" Tory walked over to the spider and picked

it up in her hand. "Come on, Robyn. It's just George. He's my buddy. He won't hurt you." She started walking slowly toward Robyn, holding the spider out for her to see.

Robyn shuddered and crouched as far back into the corner as she could get. She put her hands over her eyes and shivered. "No, no, no," she begged. "I hate spiders. Please get it out of here."

Tory immediately backed off when she saw that Robyn was sincerely afraid. Taking the spider into the next stall, she let him go. "Go do your thing, George. Fly season will soon be upon us again, and I'm counting on you."

When she got back to the tack room, Robyn was clearing the spiderweb away from the saddle and bridle. "Hey, look here," she said as she lifted a leather flap on one side of the saddle. "It's an egg sack. I don't think your friend George is a he. I believe he's a mom."

"Well, what do you know," Tory said in surprise. She picked up the egg sack and carried it into the stall where she had put the spider and placed it carefully on a crossbeam. "There you go, Georgette. I hope you can find your family again. I'd let them hatch out on my saddle, but that would mean no riding for a long time, and I couldn't handle that. I hope you understand."

Just then Robyn walked by the stall lugging the saddle in her arms. She gave Tory a funny look. "You are really weird, you know," she said with a grimace.

"I know," Tory replied. "That's why I'm friends with you."

The girls both laughed and walked out to the paddock together to find Peaches. Tory watched approvingly as Robyn caught and bridled the mare, then led her to the alley of the barn to saddle her.

"You're doing great," Tory said. "Pretty soon you'll be ready to get a horse of your own."

"I wish," Robyn said, a wistful tone in her voice. "I've wanted a horse of my own for as long as I can remember. But there's no way on just Mom's salary that we can afford to buy one. Maybe when I get out of nursing school and get a job things will be different." She pulled the cinch of Peaches' saddle up tight, then walked her in a circle to get her to let her breath out before she gave it a final tug.

Tory held the mare's reins while Robyn mounted up. "So you're going to live with your mom when you get out of school instead of getting your own apartment?"

"At least for a while. Mom has had to work so hard to support us, especially since I've been in college. I want to help out with the bills for a while to give her a chance to do something nice for herself for a change—like traveling. What are you going to do?"

Tory shrugged. "I don't know. I'm still praying about it. I'd like to do some kind of mission work, though. Something where I could work with kids."

"Sounds exciting," Robyn said, wheeling Peaches around and heading for the barrels. "This is as adventurous as I can handle for right now," she called over her shoulder as the mare galloped toward the barrels as if she'd been shot out of a gun. The cut tendon meant that Peaches could no longer jump, but she could still run.

"Ride 'em, cowgirl," Tory yelled. She started to shout another word of encouragement to her friend, but just then she turned to see her mother crossing the road to the barn lot. One look at Mrs. Butler's ashen face and she knew something was terribly wrong. Her heart twisted into a cold knot of fear.

"Mom, what is it?" she gasped.

CHAPTER FOURTEEN

Dee Butler held her hands out to Tory as she ran to meet her, tears brimming in her eyes. "It's Kane, Tory," she said, the words slicing the air between them like a knife. "Mrs. Thompson just called. There's been a terrible accident. I think he may have been killed."

Tory stopped in her tracks and stared at her mother. She tried to make some sense of what the woman had just said.

"What?" The ground seemed to sway and everything around her became a blur. "That can't be," she heard herself saying. "I just saw him in the hall at school on Friday. What are you talking about?"

Tory and Robyn moved as if in a trance, unsaddling Peaches, grooming her, and putting her away, then driving back to Robyn's house to see if they could find out any more about the accident.

Mrs. Thompson met them both at the door and wrapped her arms around them, tears streaming down her cheeks. She told the girls that she had heard the news of the accident from Kane's mother just minutes before she'd called them. Kane had been riding in a car with several other boys who had been drinking. According to a boy that survived the accident, the driver had been accelerating, trying to scare the others. As the vehicle reached a speed of more than 100 mph, the boy said Kane begged the driver to let him out of the car, but he only went faster. Suddenly they came upon a curve in the road. Traveling as fast as they were, they swung around the curve in the left-hand lane and hit an oncoming car. Only the boy who told the story survived in Kane's vehicle. A mother and three of her young children died in the other car.

Tory pulled away as a feeling of helplessness and rage boiled up inside her. "It can't be true," she shouted. "They made a mistake. It wasn't Kane, I know it wasn't. He's too young to die. He has his whole life ahead of him."

Mrs. Thompson reached for Tory's hand. Leading her to the living room, she pulled her down beside her on the sofa and held her while she sobbed. Robyn turned on the radio just as the local news began. The first story of the hour detailed the accident and listed the names of those killed. Kane's topped the list.

A strange numbness took over Tory's thoughts. She got up and walked to the window, staring out at the blue sky and the bright red geraniums growing in the Thompson's flower garden. How could life just go on like everything was normal? She wanted to scream, but felt that if she opened her mouth, no sound would come out.

He was so close to accepting You, Father. I know he was. How could You let this happen? How could such a horrible thing be Your will?

She felt Mrs. Thompson's arm around her waist. Almost as if the woman had read her thoughts, Tory heard her say, "God didn't take Kane's life, Tory. He wanted him to live, too." Her voice broke with sadness. "He never takes away our free choice, and Kane chose to be in the car with those boys who were drinking. But there's no way we can know what God may have been able to do in Kane's heart those last few minutes before the crash. We have to leave him in God's hands."

Tory buried her face in Mrs. Thompson's shoulder and cried until she felt her heart would burst with sorrow. The woman held her close, rocking her gently back and forth as if she were a little child.

"Your feelings are too raw right now to even be able to think about it," she said softly as Tory's tears subsided, "but the day will come when you will be faced with a decision. When loss rips at your heart, you eventually come up against two choices. You can harden your heart in bitterness against God and against those who caused your pain, or you can open it to God's healing, embrace the pain, and choose to forgive." She stroked Tory's hair. "Only through the second choice can you learn the lessons God has for you and really grow. I know from my own experience what I'm talking about."

Tory listened to Mrs. Thompson's words as if through a fog. Somehow, though, she sensed that they would be very important to her in the coming months. But for right now, she just tucked them away in her mind and let herself flow with the grief that carried her along.

Father, this is worse than losing Brian, she cried. *At least I know he loves You and is happy with Breeze. How I wish I had done more to help Kane see how important it was to know You.*

But she realized, even as she spoke the words in her heart, that there was nothing more she could have done. She had presented her concept of God in the best way she knew how. What Kane had decided to do with the information had been completely up to him.

With Kane gone, Tory poured herself into her studies and into Poppyseed's training. The colt grew like a weed and soon his legs were almost as long as his mother's. Every day Tory spent at least an hour handling his feet, grooming him, and reinforcing the basics of leading, backing, and trailering. And every day, she was amazed all over again at the colt's gentle disposition and eagerness to obey her.

Summer passed, with its flurry of gardening, canning, and freezing. Tory laughed as her father brought the hundredth zucchini into the house and her mother, usually so soft-spoken, shouted, "I don't ever want to see another one of those horrible vegetables as long as I live."

Even the hummingbirds seemed to be trying to stay as busy as possible, flitting from feeder to feeder as if trying to drain them dry before winter set in. "I think I need to start buying sugar by the boxcar load," Mrs. Butler joked. "I've never seen so many hungry little dynamos."

The crisp days of fall brought with them a feeling of deep sadness for Tory as she remembered flying with Kane and the times they walked through the colorful leaves to her secret place beside the waterfall.

"I don't think I'll ever get over this," she told Robyn one day as they rode Peaches double out across the fields, Poppyseed prancing along beside them. "I miss him so much. How long does it take to start feeling better?"

"I guess they say you'll never completely heal," Robyn said thoughtfully. "There will always be scars, although time is supposed to help with the pain. I know that doesn't help much."

Tory shook her head. "You know, sometimes I think that if the pain went away, I might forget how much I cared about Kane. So I guess I don't mind if the pain hangs around for a while." She made a face. "It's funny, because I knew that if Kane didn't surrender his life to God, we couldn't be together anyway. Even if he were still alive, I would have had to face the pain of losing him."

Later that week, while Tory was studying for a nursing test, the phone rang. She kept studying, letting her mother answer it.

"It's for you," she heard Mrs. Butler call from the kitchen. When she walked out of her room, her mother stood in the hallway, holding the cordless phone, a strange look on her face. "It's someone from Michigan. I've never heard of them before," she whispered, holding her hand over the receiver. "Who in the world would be calling you from Michigan?"

Tory shrugged and took the phone.

"Hello, Tory?" The voice on the line had a thick accent. "This is Anna Giles from Outreach, International. We build and operate orphanages all over the world. Someone gave us your name, saying that you are interested in mission work, and we have a need for someone with medical training to help with the children in one of our facilities in Central America. Would you be willing to go?"

Tory took a deep breath. "Uh, well, I'm not done with school. I have several months to go, and I'm really not sure what I'm going to do." She paused, her thoughts scrambling over each other in confusion. "How did you say you got my name?"

"A friend of yours recommended you. Her name was Robyn Thompson."

Tory looked helplessly at her mom, who stood staring at her, obviously curious as to the nature of the call. "May I have your number?" she asked, motioning to Mrs. Butler to hand her a pen and paper. "I'd like to think about this and phone you back."

"Certainly," the woman said.

Tory wrote down the number, then hung up the phone.

"Whew!" she said, throwing her hands up in the air. "It's amazing how life can change completely in just a few seconds." She gave the piece of paper to her mother. "It's a mission opportunity. Robyn turned my name in. I'd be working with children, just like I've always wanted to do. Do you think this is something God wants me to do?"

Mrs. Butler shook her head. "That's something you'd have to pray about and decide between you and God. I wouldn't even try to influence you. Mission life is hard, and you have to be sure that God is calling you and that you're ready to make the sacrifices it takes."

That night, as Tory snuggled down under her covers, she reached for the Bible on her nightstand. *Father, guide my thoughts. Help me to know Your plans for me. Should I go to this orphanage to work for You, or is there somewhere else You want me to be?* She opened her Bible and read Matthew 28. As she came to the verses that described Jesus' ascension into heaven, she caught her breath. It was as if the words jumped from the page, a message just for her. In her heart she could hear Jesus saying to her, "Go and make disciples of all nations, baptizing them in the name of the Father and of the Son and of the Holy Spirit, and teaching them to obey everything I have commanded you."

Suddenly she remembered a spiritual gifts test she had taken several years earlier that had revealed one of her strongest gifts, besides those of mercy and teaching, as the gift of missions. She knew she loved studying other cultures, trying to understand the worldviews of others in different surroundings and with different belief systems than her own, but she had never dreamed the opportunity to serve in a mission setting would come so soon.

Father, You're asking me to go, aren't You? Tory's eyes filled with tears at the thought of such an honor. *Well, my answer is yes.*

Turning out the light beside her bed, she lay staring at the darkened ceiling, wondering what changes in her life her decision would bring. She realized that it meant leaving her parents, but she knew they had expected her to go somewhere else to work when she graduated anyway. Then Poppyseed flashed into her mind. The horses! What would she do with the horses?

Thinking of giving Poppyseed's training over to someone else sent a stab of pain through her heart, but she knew there would be no way to take him with her. She turned toward the wall and pulled the covers up over her head.

I'm going to leave that detail with You, Father. It's too much for me to handle right now, she prayed. And with that she went to sleep.

CHAPTER FIFTEEN

Tory straightened her graduation cap as she stood in the long line of students waiting for "Pomp and Circumstances" to play so they could march to the front of the auditorium. She turned around to see Robyn, almost at the end of the line, waving frantically at her. She chuckled as Robyn pulled up her graduation gown to reveal jeans underneath instead of the elegant dresses many of the other girls were wearing.

Tory had chosen a simple cotton sundress to wear today. Even though it was still fairly cool at 9:00 a.m., she knew the temperature would soar by noon when the group would be standing around outside posing for the endless round of picture-taking that always accompanied such special events.

The music began, and she moved slowly with the group, step by step, in time with the majestic harmony. She spotted her parents, sitting with Mrs. Thompson, near the front of the auditorium. They waved and smiled proudly. Tory waved back, feeling a surge of gratitude for the way they had supported her the past several years.

"You should be the ones getting this diploma," she whispered as she blew them a kiss.

The ceremony over, they all stood out on the lawn while Mr. Butler snapped pictures of the girls in their hats and gowns, holding their diplomas.

"Smile pretty, ladies," Mrs. Thompson called from her place in the shade of an old oak. "These are for posterity."

Just then a strange man walked across the lawn toward them. "Well, I've got something for my posterity," he said in a deep, booming voice. With that, he grabbed Robyn and gave her a bear hug.

"Daddy!" the girl shrieked. "I didn't know you were coming. Were you here for the whole thing? Did you see me get my diploma?"

Tory glanced over at Mrs. Thompson, still standing under the tree, and noticed the smile of pleasure on her face at seeing her daughter so happy. Even when Mr. Thompson's new wife joined them, and everybody made introductions around the circle, Mrs. Thompson treated the woman with graciousness and respect. Tory thought back to the story Robyn had told her about her mother's struggle with bitterness against her ex-husband and against the woman he married. How could her attitude have changed so much toward the people who had hurt her the most in life?

Then, as if in a dream, she remembered the day of Kane's death and Mrs. Thompson's words to her as she cried in her arms. *You can harden your heart in bitterness against those who caused your pain, or you can open it to God's healing, embrace the pain, and choose to forgive.* She realized as she watched the woman interact with Christlike love and concern for her "ex" and his wife, that she truly had chosen to forgive.

"Come on over to our house, all of you," Mrs. Butler said, when they had used up the last roll of film. "We have graduation dinner all prepared, just waiting for a crowd of hungry people to eat it."

Both of the Thompson families accepted the invitation. As the group piled into cars for the drive to the Butlers, Tory noticed that Robyn chose to ride with her mother instead of in her father's jeep. She was glad to see her friend being so sensitive to her mother's feelings.

Tory and Robyn helped Mrs. Butler get the meal on the table while Mr. Butler took the Thompsons on a tour of the farm. Tory placed bowls of fluffy mashed potatoes, steaming gravy, corn, green beans, and coleslaw on the table. A huge cake with the words "Congratulations graduates" written on it in blue and gold frosting sat on the counter.

"This is so exciting," Robyn said with a dramatic sigh. "All we have to do now is pass our licensing exam, and we'll be real honest-to-goodness nurses." She wrinkled up her nose. "O-o-h. Scary thought, huh?"

Tory nodded, her eyes wide. "It especially scares me that I'll be working in a country where I don't even speak the language."

"So you've decided to go for sure?" Mrs. Thompson said, walking in the door just in time to hear Tory's last statement.

"Yes, I have," the girl answered slowly. "The arrangements are all made." She looked at Robyn. "All of them except one, that is."

Robyn raised her eyebrows questioningly. "I thought you told me everything was in place. What else do you have to do?"

"I need to adopt my children out," Tory said, keeping her voice serious and her face straight.

"What?" Robyn stared at her. "You don't have any children. Unless you're talking about the children at the orphanage, and you can't start adopting them out before you even get there."

With a laugh Tory said, "Can you both come outside with me? I need to ask you something." She looked at her mother and the two exchanged knowing looks. Mrs. Butler nodded.

Tory led Robyn and Mrs. Thompson out to the paddock where Poppyseed and Peaches stood munching on a sheaf of hay. Poppyseed's sleek black coat shone in the warm sunlight, and he stood almost as tall as his mother.

"That has got to be the world's most beautiful colt," Mrs. Thompson said. She held out her hand to Poppyseed, and he walked over to the fence, nosing her hand curiously. "I wish I could afford to get a horse like this for Robyn. There's nothing she's wanted more through the years. And there's nothing I would have rather done for her as she was growing up." Her face looked wistful as she patted the colt's neck.

Tory cleared her throat. "Well. That's kind of along the lines of what I wanted to ask you," she said. "There's no one in the world that I would trust more with Poppyseed's training and with Peaches' care than you, Robyn."

Mrs. Thompson and Robyn both stood and stared at Tory. "What are you saying?" Robyn asked, a look of amazement on her face as her friend's words began to sink in.

"I want you to take my horses," Tory said. "I've already talked this over with my parents. They don't have the time or the inclination to work with Poppyseed. He needs to continue his education, and Peaches needs to be ridden to stay in shape." She paused to take a breath, then plunged on. "I know you can't buy them and that's OK. Would you be willing to keep them for me until I can come back and get them? I don't have any idea how long that will be."

Mrs. Thompson turned to look at Robyn, her eyes

sparkling with excitement. "Well, sis," she said, grinning. "Do you want to do it?"

"Are you kidding?" Robyn gasped. "And have a lifelong dream come true?"

Tory chuckled. "I take it that's a yes?"

"Yes. Yes. Yes. Yes, it's a yes," Robyn shouted, performing a little Indian dance on the spot where she stood.

Later that evening, after the party was over and the guests had gone home, Tory stood in the purple shadows that crept along the edges of the pasture as the sun sank over the trees in the west. Peaches grazed contentedly on a clump of new clover that had sprung up near the creek. Poppyseed lay sprawled in the waning sunlight, soaking up the still-warm rays with his dark coat.

Tory thought back to her first day home when her father had given Peaches to her as a gift.

"So much has changed for us, hasn't it, girl," she whispered. "That's what life is all about, isn't it? Change." She thought of Kane and realized that knowing him had transformed her forever. Never again would she take a friendship for granted. She thought of her decision to go to Central America to work with the orphanage there and realized that that decision had altered her, too. It was as if her commitment to God had somehow deepened and grown, and she found herself more willing to trust Him with her future.

She watched Poppyseed stand up and shake the dust from his coat. He nickered when he saw Tory and trotted toward her, his delicate ears perked forward in interest. As he reached her, he nuzzled her cheek affectionately.

"Oh, Poppyseed," Tory cried, burying her face in his mane. "How can I leave you? You are like my very own child."

The colt stood quietly while Tory hugged him, trying to absorb his smell and the feel of his soft coat so that whatever happened in the future, she would have those memories with her.

I trust You, Father, she prayed, running her fingers through the soft curls of the colt's mane. *I know you'll take care of Poppyseed, just like You've taken care of me.*

The sun sank behind the hilltops, an orange ball of flames. Tory kissed Poppyseed on the nose and turned to go. The colt ran after her as she walked away, as if he sensed the finality of the moment.

"No," Tory said, tears blinding her eyes. "You stay with your mom. She needs you and so does Robyn. You guys will do great things together."

Climbing through the fence, she walked up the road, cutting off into the woods on her secret path, drawn by the faint tinkling of the little waterfall. She sat on the rock where she and Kane had spent so many hours talking, and where she'd spent so much time in prayer, asking for direction as she wrestled with decisions about her future. Watching the little waterfall, she focused in on individual droplets of water as they hurled themselves off the rocks and down into the pool below.

I'm like one of those little drops, aren't I, Father? she whispered. *And You are the riverbed, solid and sure, carrying me along to a future I can't see. I choose to trust you with it. Always.*

A cool breeze caressed Tory's face as she stood and started up the path toward home, and she knew in her heart that she had just made the best choice of her life.

GLOSSARY OF HORSEMANSHIP TERMS

barrel The trunk of a horse, the area between the fore- and hindquarters.

bay A horse of medium-brown color with a black mane and tail.

bedding Materials used to cover the floor of a stall, such as straw, peat moss, or wood shavings.

blaze A wide white mark running from between the eyes down to the muzzle.

breastplate Leather piece across a horse's chest that attaches to the saddle and the girth to prevent the saddle from slipping back.

breed Any horse with a distinct bloodline that can be traced through a registry, such as Arab, Thoroughbred, and Morgan.

bridle A head harness used to control a horse and usually including a bit, reins, crownpiece, cheek straps, throatlatch, headband, and noseband.

buckskin A beige color with a black mane and tail, sometimes black points and dorsal and eel stripes.

canter A slow gallop, a three-beat gait originally called the Canterbury gallop.

cantle The rear of the saddle.

chestnut A color similar to bronze or copper, often referred to in the West as "sorrel."

cinch The girth of a Western saddle.

colic A painful, sometimes fatal stomach ailment usually caused by overeating, overheating, or overwork.

colt A male horse under the age of 4.

conformation The way a horse is built.

cooling off Walking a horse after exercise to prevent colic and founder.

crest The area on the top of a horse's neck.

crownpiece The part of the bridle that goes over the horse's head and attaches to the cheekpieces.

curb A type of bit used when the rider needs more control of the horse.

curb chain A chain or strap used under the horse's chin to provide pressure when the rider pulls the reins.

dam A horse's mother.

dapple A spotted pattern that blends into the horse's coat, as opposed to an Appa-loosa's spot pattern, which consists of distinct spots.

draft horse A horse originally bred to do farm work. Very large build.

dun A flat, brownish-beige color with a mane and tail of the same color.

filly A female horse under the age of 4.

flaxen Chestnut with white or cream-colored mane and tail.

floating The filing down of rough teeth to give them a smooth surface.

foal A newborn filly or colt.

forehand The front quarters of a horse, including the head, neck, shoulders, and front legs.

forelock Hair from the horse's mane that hangs down between the ears.

founder Swelling of the inside of a horse's foot. In some cases the sole of the foot separates from the wall. It results from overfeeding, overheating, and overworking.

gallop The fastest of the speeds or "gaits" of a horse.

gelding A castrated or gelded male horse or pony.

girth The leather band that encircles the horse's body to hold the saddle in place.

ground tie A method by which a horse is taught to stand still when its rider dismounts and drops the end of one rein on the ground.

halter A headpiece consisting of a noseband, cheek strap, and headband used for tying or leading a horse.

hand A standard of measurement for horses. Four inches equals one hand. A horse is measured by hands from the bottom of the front hoof to the top of the withers.

headband The part of the bridle that goes over the horse's forehead.

headstall All the parts of the bridle except the bit and reins.

hindquarters The part of the horse behind the barrel.

leading Walking a horse forward by standing at its shoulder with the reins or lead rope in your right hand, and moving your left foot in unison with his right leg.

lope Same as canter; a slow, balanced, three-beat gait.

mare A full-grown female horse.

muzzle The part of the horse's head that includes the nose, nostrils, lips, and chin.

neck rein Turning the horse by laying the reins across the side of the neck to turn in the opposite direction.

noseband The part of the bridle that goes over the horse's nose.

paddock A small, fenced area that adjoins the barn so the horse can go in and out at will.

piebald A black and white horse. Sometimes called a pinto.

points The color of the muzzle, legs, mane, and tail.

poll The part of the horse's neck behind the ears, the highest point.

pommel The front part of the saddle.

pony Any horse under 14.2 hands tall.

quarter horse A breed developed to race short distances. Muscular and stocky.

roan A coloration that is either bay, black, or chestnut sprinkled throughout with white hairs to give it a frosted appearance.

shank A lead line of half leather or rope and half chain.

sire The father of a horse.

snip A white mark on a horse's nostrils.

sock White on the leg below the fetlock joint.

spook A tendency in the horse to shy and bolt for no apparent reason.

stallion A mature male horse used for breeding.

star A small, white mark between a horse's eyes.

stocking White on the leg from the knee down.

tack Any equipment used in riding and handling a horse.

throatlatch The strap on the bridle that goes under the throat.

tree The frame inside the saddle.

trot A two-beat gait where the horse's legs move diagonally.

walk A natural slow four-beated gait.

weanling A foal that has been weaned and is not yet a yearling.